Praise for Sheil

"Sheila Kohler has written a slyly sub
revisionist interpretation of Sigmund
case that might be subtitled 'The An.

—Joyce Carol Oates, *New York Times* bestselling
author of *We Were the Mulvaneys*

"With delicate and terrifying grace Kohler illuminates the complex hidden lives of her characters, whose needs and desires transgress the bounds of the familiar and comfortable. This seductive and wonderfully unexpected tale confirms Sheila Kohler's place as a master of the novel."

—A. M. Homes (on *The Bay of Foxes*),
author of *May We Be Forgiven*

"Sheila Kohler's prose smokes and burns like a fire that cannot be put out and that suddenly leaps into all-devouring flame. She has all the gifts of a natural storyteller—a passionate interest in human motives, an eidetic recall of period and place, and a sense of the shape of a tale unfolding in the fullness of time."

—Edmund White, author of *City Boy* and *Genet*

"Sheila Kohler possesses a gorgeous imagination."

—Patrick McGrath, author of *Trauma*

"Sheila Kohler's timeless stories are always transporting. The elegance of her writing underscores the charged, disturbing behavior she presents so vividly."

—Amy Hempel, author of *The Dog of the Marriage*

"Sheila Kohler is a gifted storyteller, as this her latest attests. *Dreaming for Freud* is well crafted, depicting two great strong-willed characters: the forty-five-year-old Sigmund Freud and the feisty seventeen-year-old patient he made famous as Dora. Kohler reveals her secrets slowly, layer by layer, teaching us much about the early days of Freud's 'talking cure.' Like any good mystery writer, she keeps us suspended until the very end. This is a compelling and very satisfying read."

—Selden Edwards, author of *The Lost Prince*

"In this meticulously researched novel, Kohler infuses Freud's case report of his analysis of Dora with a richly imagined, entirely credible reading between the lines. Her effortless prose is powerfully evocative of the characters, the times, and the essence of the unique relationship that we call psychoanalysis."

—David I. Joseph, MD, George Washington
Department of Psychiatry and Behavioral Sciences

"*Dreaming for Freud* is an extraordinary novel that focuses on one of Freud's seminal cases involving a highly intelligent, sensitive young woman that contributed to a tectonic shift in the science of psychodynamics and psychiatry in general. In this mesmerizing work, Kohler brilliantly constructs fascinating dialogue between Freud and his patient, but even more interesting, excursions into their minds, which reveal their ambivalences, vulnerabilities, and power plays."

—Laurence R. Tancredi, MD, JD,
Clinical Professor of Psychiatry, New York University

"Compelling and beautifully nuanced."

—Elizabeth Strout (on *Crossways*), author of *Olive Kitteridge*

"Kohler is undoubtedly a talent to watch."   —*Vogue*

"Hypnotic . . . unsettling . . . a combination of domestic drama and psychological thriller."

—*San Francisco Chronicle* (on *Crossways*)

"Her themes of displacement and alienation cut to the heart as she quietly strips away the tales we tell ourselves in order to go on from day to day."   —*Booklist*

"Patricia Highsmith meets Nadine Gordimer in this mesmerizing tale of sex, longing, and murder."

—Jonathan Santlofer (on *The Bay of Foxes)*, author of *The Death Artist*

"Bravo! I couldn't put it down and finished it in the depths of the night."   —Lyndall Gordon (on *Becoming Jane Eyre*), author of *Charlotte Brontë: A Passionate Life*

"Erotic and disturbing."   —*Vanity Fair* (on *Cracks*)

"Riveting . . . Kohler's writing is so smoothly confident and erotic that she has produced a tale resonant with a chilling power all its own."   —*Elle* (on *Cracks*)

"Spare, haunting."   —*Marie Claire* (on *Cracks*)

"Her writing is precise, colorful, and sensual . . . expertly paced. Kohler has produced a masterful narrative."

—*Atlanta Journal-Constitution* (on *Crossways*)

DREAMING FOR FREUD

A NOVEL

SHEILA KOHLER

PENGUIN BOOKS

PENGUIN BOOKS
Published by the Penguin Group
Penguin Group (USA) LLC
375 Hudson Street
New York, New York 10014

USA | Canada | UK | Ireland | Australia
New Zealand | India | South Africa | China
penguin.com

A Penguin Random House Company

First published in Penguin Books 2014

Extracts from Freud's *Fragment of an Analysis of a Case of Hysteria*,
Standard Edition, Volume VII,
translated from the German by William Tucker.

LIBRARY OF CONGRESS CATALOGING-IN-PUBLICATION DATA
Kohler, Sheila.
Dreaming for Freud : a novel / Sheila Kohler.
pages cm
ISBN 978-0-14-312519-8
I. Title.
PR9369.3.K64D84 2014
823'.914—dc23   2013048717

Printed in the United States of America
1   3   5   7   9   10   8   6   4   2

Set in Bembo Std   •   Designed by Elke Sigal

This is a work of fiction based on real events.

For my best—my husband, Bill Tucker

How can we know the dancer from the dance?

—WILLIAM BUTLER YEATS

DREAMING FOR FREUD

JANUARY 2, 1901

I

BEREFT

HE SITS AT HIS DESK in his study, sucking on his cigar. It is late, and his family is already in bed, which is where he should be, but instead he picks up and puts down the Egyptian, Greek, and Roman statuettes before him, bought at some sacrifice, which only makes them more precious. He began this collection shortly after the death of his father and after dreaming a series of dreams about Rome, four years ago, as though mourning had sent him on a voyage of discovery, searching for memories in an underworld linked to the beginnings of things. He is irresistibly attracted to this world of ancient things, studying, buying, rearranging. He finds handling these small, light objects strangely comforting— sometimes he even takes them with him to the table at mealtimes—and he is much in need of comfort tonight, moving them around restlessly at will. He cannot stop thinking about the case.

Just when the treatment seemed to be going so well, just when he was analyzing the girl's dreams with what he can only feel was considerable understanding and expertise, just when he was breaking through her hysterical resistance, the girl has, to his consternation, broken off the treatment, refused to come back. This slip of a girl who had come to him in the autumn of the first year of the century, in his forty-fourth year, has escaped him.

She has left him with nothing but a fragment of an analysis in his hands. Not given sufficient time, he has been unable to explore her case fully and to his satisfaction. He thinks with a dull ache that like all the rest ultimately, and young as she is, this woman will remain a dark continent. Once again he has failed with a patient. His dreams of finding gold in the heart of her story have not been realized. He is strangely troubled by this abrupt departure, which he is aware must recall earlier and even more painful leave-takings. The origin of all this heartache lies in the past, he knows.

He stubs out his half-finished cigar, rises, and walks back and forth over the Persian carpets, his hands behind his back. As his favorite sister, Rosa, with her husband and two small children, has the apartment opposite his on the second floor, he has been obliged to move his study and consulting rooms downstairs.

He looks at his empty ottoman, draped with its soft Smyrna rug, and thinks he would like to tell his friend Fliess how the girl has fled, will never come back and lie down here. She will never plump herself down and lean against the large, plush pillows, as though she owned the place. Despite all his efforts to create as much of an impression of comfort as he has had the means to do within these small, modest rooms, she has left him for good. This place where he has brought up his family seems empty; three of his six children were born in this house—his youngest girl, Anna, is five years old.

Looking around the crowded, dimly lit interior, he remembers floating through his great master Charcot's vast and elegant rooms in Paris fifteen years ago, high on cocaine. Here he has no such elegance, nor the comfort of the drug, but he does have his ancient statuettes and his books. He has been reading Burckhardt's famous book, *The Civilization of the Renaissance in Italy.* He has tried to give his patients an illusion of reassuring permanence, a sense of eternity evoked by the past, something that will mirror the solidity of this brilliant, bourgeois Viennese world and even the vast empire beyond, with its apparently immortal emperor, the ancient Franz Joseph, who has been on the throne now for more than fifty years, ever since he replaced his idiot uncle in 1848. A stable world, he would like to believe, everything in its well-appointed place, a world of flourishing science and arts; of music, literature, theater, and painting, a world where his own Jewish people have played such a prominent part.

Many years later he will think back on the irony of these paltry attempts to portray a solid world. He will cling to this illusion until the last moment—until his own daughter has been rounded up and taken from him twice by the Gestapo and held for a whole day—unable to imagine it shattering, coming to an abrupt end in the new century. Though there was never a time in his life when he was not aware of the hatred for his people, he will not be able to imagine what this orderly space will become. How can he imagine the suffering that will take place in this bourgeois room, a room that will be copied again and again all over the world by budding analysts in search of legitimacy?

What he now sees so clearly in his mind, the image coming to him repeatedly in the silence and loneliness of the late hour, is his young patient as he last saw her, waving her slender, white hands in the air. She is a girl who uses her hands expressively when she speaks. He can hear the chink of her many gold bracelets and see her large, lucent eyes fill with tears as she stands at the door in her white dress—she often wears white—and presses his hand warmly between hers. "I will be back to see you, one day, I'm sure," she tells him, which he takes for a white lie. In any case he is determined never to take her back should she really want to come. Her voice trembles a little, her long lashes lowered to her cheeks, as she says good-bye and wishes him and his family a very happy new year.

Yet the termination of the analysis is, he feels, an act of revenge on her part. She must have realized how important her case had become to him. She has dismissed him, he thinks bitterly, with little notice, rather like a maid, or come to think of it, like his own adored Catholic nursemaid who was so abruptly dismissed for stealing. This girl, he feels, has stolen something precious from him.

All that is left to him now, he realizes, as he walks back and forth in the silence of the late hour, snow falling softly outside his window in the courtyard with its one tall chestnut tree, is to write up his account of the treatment. This will have to be *his* revenge. He will put aside the important work he has begun on the psychology of everyday life. He will leave the chapter about forgetting the name of Signorelli, the painter, and turn to the writing of this case. Its very brevity, the three months she has allowed him, he sees, with a sudden surge of hope, may be used to his advantage. The short time span will contain it; it will help him structure the account. He has not been able to write up the account of the longer and more complete analysis of Herr E. She has done him a favor, in a way, he suddenly sees.

A vague idea of how he will do it comes to him: it will have five parts perhaps, with an explanatory preface at the start and the two important dreams placed toward the end, just before the postscript.

He sits down again at his desk, puts aside the ancient statuettes, sweeps away the manuscript he was working on, and takes up a clean sheet of paper. He writes in a sort of fever. He needs to get it all down while the details are still fresh in his mind. He wants to demonstrate how dream interpretation elucidates an entire analysis, pointing the way through the formidable resistance of all hysterics. This will be the necessary continuation of his dream book as well as his earlier studies in hysteria. The two dreams she has brought him will be all the gold required.

Also, he is aware that he needs to express his thoughts in writing to understand this hysterical girl at least as much as he can, to reveal her to himself as much as to others, to relive on the page the moments he has spent with her despite all her rudeness and recalcitrance. Though he has never re-corded their exchanges, except for her dreams, which he did write down—the most important part of the analysis—he has his nightly notes and remembers many of her exact words. They reverberate in his mind. Indeed, he finds himself re-peating some of the things *he* has said to her aloud, aware of his lips.

"Why would you not trust me? I will trust you to tell me the truth," he says aloud. "And can you be so sure we did not?" he repeats his last words to her. At forty-four he be-lieves he still has a good enough memory, though it is not what it used to be when he was an adolescent and could re-member pages of text by heart.

Despite his haste to record the analysis, he writes care-fully, in what he is aware is a forceful and compelling style. He possesses the gift of going directly from his ex-perience to the word. He has always seen things clearly, known how to seize on the essential and render it intelligible and convincing to his reader. He has learned a lot from his French master, Charcot. He knows how to simplify and clarify.

For the moment he does not ask himself who will read this account, or even if his admired Fliess, his Other, will consent to critique it, as he did his book on dreams. Though he knows it is impossible for him to write without hope of some audience, he now writes for himself as much as his fu-ture readers. He writes out of a desire to put this bright girl down on the page, to understand their interaction, to hold on to her in the stillness of the night, to possess her forever through the written word. Posterity will know her only through his eyes, he believes.

He will have to rename her, of course, and a perfect name comes to him immediately, as though waiting in the wings. It is the name they used for his sister's maid, her given name, Rosa, having led to a confusion between mistress and maid. She will be cast in the role of the maid, not he. He is vaguely aware that it is also the name of a helpless child bride from a beloved novel by his favorite English writer, as well as one from a play he saw once in Paris about a Roman empress, a woman of great power and intrigue. He knows, too, that it is the name of the woman who opened up the box and let all the evils out into the world.

He will disguise the places where she has lived, too, and the people she has known. He will disguise her story just enough, and all in the name of scientific research, in the name of the truth.

As he begins to set down his account, he realizes he is inventing the girl, giving her a new life and substance, as he explains the reasons for her symptoms. Ultimately, he feels, she will now belong to *him*.

She will never refute his interpretations. Despite her unusual intelligence, her willfulness and recalcitrance, she will always be his creation. He will confer immortality on her and further science with his brilliant analysis, and if, in the future, she should hear of her fame, he suspects she may be proud. She is a proud girl.

And how many other readers might find themselves in these pages? How many hysterical adolescent girls will find their desires exposed, their masks removed? It will be his revenge not just on this one lively, pretty, bright girl who has dared to scorn him, but on all of them with their dangerous charms. It will be his revenge on all his enemies, his hypocritical Viennese colleagues who have snubbed him and his dream book, who have refused to see the truth of what is so clearly before their eyes.

OCTOBER 1900

———

I I

FATHER AND DAUGHTER

SHE HESITATES AT THE TOP of the stairs, looking down at her father. She can hear the early afternoon sounds: the vague hum of the servants in the kitchen washing dishes, the whistling of a sad Viennese song as the swing door into the kitchen swishes open and closed; the clip-clop of a horse's hooves on the slippery, wet street. The smell of schnitzel hangs in the air.

Her father preens himself like a peacock before the gold-framed mirror in the dark hall. Covering his mouth, he yawns sleepily after his copious luncheon, while she has eaten nothing at all, unable to touch the heavy food in the dark dining room despite his encouragement. He has his gray silk hat in one kid-gloved hand and smooths his thick hair back with the other. She considers him an elegant man, with something soft, almost feminine about his face, as though the thin mustache were an afterthought. She recognizes the slightly prominent ears she has inherited and wonders what else she might have inherited from him.

He is a vain man, too. He knows everyone finds him

handsome, particularly the ladies, except, ironically, his wife, who seems more interested in cleaning the house. All the other ladies like the thick, auburn, slightly curly hair, the wide-spaced dark blue eyes, the svelte, boyish form. Everyone remarks on his charm, intelligence, and considerable business acumen. She is a very fortunate girl, who should be happy and not sad, or so everyone tells her, which only makes her feel worse.

Despite all her advantages, she does not feel fortunate as she stands with her hand on the highly polished banister at the top of the green carpeted stairs in her expensive white dress. She knows she should feel grateful for the education she has received: the foreign languages, French, English, a little Italian, the Czech her parents speak; the petit point; the piano, the drawing, the dancing lessons, the horseback riding. Instead, at seventeen, she feels old. Her youth and vitality have already vanished. Her young body has betrayed her. She feels it is leaking bitterness from all its orifices. Her body is weeping, and it is the fault of this man who stands before the mirror: her false, false father! She cannot bear his falseness. He lies to her. Everyone knows he does. Yet he tells her *she* lies. But no one says anything. This silence in the household is driving her mad.

She will always love him—how could she not? she thinks, watching him admire himself, turning his big, handsome head sideways to the mirror, tilting his dimpled chin at an advantageous angle. Yet she is in a rage with him. She feels at this moment if she could let something heavy drop directly onto his head—which, from her viewpoint, seems slightly too large for his slender body—and shatter his skull into a million pieces, she would. *She would!*

He has insisted she return to see his doctor. As if it will do any good! At breakfast a few days ago, sitting at the table alone with him—her brother had already left for the university, and her mother had not put in an appearance—she was overcome with a fit of coughing. He lay down *Die Fackel*—the newspaper he reads from cover to cover, with all the headlines about the Hilsner case. He said, "We have to get to the bottom of all of this." For a moment she thought he was referring to the poor murdered Catholic girl or even the poor simple-minded Jew, Hilsner, who had been accused of killing the girl to obtain blood to make *matzo*, but of course he was not talking about the hatred of the Jews at all.

Despite her irregular education she knows all about this, as one does about a fire that runs beneath the surface of things at all times, half-hidden but erupting dangerously and surprisingly at moments such as the burning of her father's textile factory a few years ago in Bohemia, or the accession of Lueger, that crafty man who has used Jew-baiting to become mayor of Vienna finally, despite the old emperor's efforts, or even her brother's stories of the way Jewish students are treated at the university. It is such an integral part of her—like her own shadow—that it is not necessary to speak of it. She has always lived with it, part of the city, the Prater, the cafés. But what her father was speaking about, of course, was not that but his own daughter's cough and all her other ailments.

"I don't understand what's the matter with you. You have everything in the world: all this hard-won security I have worked for all my life," he said, making a sweeping gesture toward the laden table, the polished sideboard with all its shining silver, the mirror with the invitations stuck into the sides, the blue silk curtains tied back with gold ropes, the broad servant's back as she retreated into the kitchens with the silver coffeepot. "You have never lacked for anything, and though we don't live extravagantly, we have always given you everything you wanted. You had a fancy French governess to teach you whatever you wished to learn, a woman you professed to love, whom we dismissed when you asked us to. What more could you possibly want? Why so much unhappiness? What is it that is missing in your young life?"

She said nothing, just went on coughing helplessly.

"I want you to go back and see my doctor," he said firmly, fixing her with his deep blue stare.

She could only shake her head and continue coughing, that awful, dry cough that shakes her whole body and takes her breath away.

"What have you got to lose?" her father had said.

"I won't go! I won't! Why would I? None of them have any idea what they are doing. Doctors! Humbugs!" she said scornfully, finding her voice in her anger at the thought of the pack of them. "They know nothing! They all say something different. They just torture me!" She put her hand to her throat, recalling the dreadful electric brush thrust into it, the electric shocks all through her body, the blast of the cold hose, the dunkings in cold baths.

"My dearest girl, you really cannot go on like this," her father said, looking at her with concern across the jars of golden honey, homemade strawberry jam and marmalade, the big pat of yellow butter, the scrambled eggs, the bright bowl of fruit, the loaves of half-cut dark bread, while he drummed his fingers on the starched white tablecloth impatiently. She sipped some ice water, which sometimes helped a little with the cough.

Many years later, having left Austria and escaped to Brooklyn, she will remember those Viennese breakfasts and miss that delicious dark bread, but that day she was not thinking of food.

She said, "I won't have anyone else sticking electric rods down my throat as if I were a cow and making me vomit, or showering me with freezing water. What good has that done!"

"He's not going to use electricity on you, I assure you, my dearest girl. He doesn't use it, or even hypnosis anymore," her father said, waving his fine hands in the air and adding, "He has an entirely new method for curing illness."

"None of it does any good," she said, pushing away her plate of scrambled eggs, the sight of which made her feel ill. This conversation made her feel ill. Her father made her feel ill.

He said, "You are a highly intelligent girl, dearest. For goodness sake, be reasonable and take advantage of the advances of modern medicine and an excellent opportunity to get well." Looking down at his hands with the gold signet ring on his pinkie, he added, "This doctor has helped me, as you well know, when I was so . . ." he looks at her and hesitates before going on, ". . . so ill." Surely he does not need to remind her of the time his mind was disordered and his body paralyzed.

"I won't go! I won't!" she replied, getting up and rushing to quit the room, her silk skirt, her favorite—she has elegant clothes, her father has been generous with her there—catching against her chair and turning it over with a clatter onto the highly polished parquet floor. She left her father sitting there alone with all the food. Sometimes, leaving people or places of danger is all you can do, she knows even then.

But in the end, she had had no choice. Her only recourse is to dally, to take her time, at the top of the stairs.

Her mother is usually the one who takes her to the doctor, or the doctor comes to the house. Despite the many servants, her mother spends her days in the house, cleaning. Her father complains she is obsessed with housecleaning and leaves her daughter's education up to the fräulein. The French fräulein, whom she once liked so much, used to bring the doctor into the nursery in Meran. Since they moved back to Vienna two years ago, and now that she is almost eighteen—her birthday is next month—she is allowed to sleep alone in her narrow bed, where she can hear the sound of the trains in the night. She occupies the room at the top of the stairs, a pale bedroom with pale-pink walls and a pale-pink, chintz-covered armchair, a pink lamp with little tassels, her small, light marquetry desk by the window with its secret drawer where she keeps her diary.

Her brilliant brother, Otto, whom she loves so much, and who will one day be famous as a successful Socialist politician and minister of foreign affairs, now sleeps meekly in a room down the corridor that is only accessible through the dining room, which their mother, who is the only one with keys, locks at night.

Her father rarely came into the nursery when she was a child. It was she who went into his sickroom, where he lay in partial darkness. But she remembers him entering once, summoned by the nanny or perhaps even by her mother. She was quite small and had done something bad.

In those days, she was a wild child, full of herself and free, running through the Vienna Woods barefoot in summer in a gauzy, smocked dress with her nanny in tow, looking for wild herbs, especially the *Tausendgüldenkraut*, a tiny pink blossom, so difficult to find. That day in the nursery, her father had thought only he could adequately punish such a crime. She was only four or five and does not recall what the punishment or the crime was, but she does remember her father coming out of the nursery holding her in his arms. She was weeping or laughing hysterically, perhaps both, but she knows he lifted her firmly aloft in his arms, and set her on his shoulders.

Today it is October and already cool and damp, with hints of winter in the air. She has pinned a little black shawl around her shoulders, and is obliged to accompany her father to the doctor's house on Berggasse, a few minutes away. It is the street where she was born. Her father waits for her impatiently, opening up his gold fob watch.

He must feel her watching him, for he looks up and sees her at the top of the stairs and smiles his lopsided, slightly ironic smile. He pulls at his gray gloves. He says, "Ah, there you are, my dear. Come along now, will you. We are already late." But she takes her time on the stairs, beating out a rhythm on the shiny banister with her slim wrist: *one-two-three, one-two-three*. She drags her right leg. She is not certain whether she is exaggerating the limp or whether she really cannot walk properly. She feels like the little mermaid in Grimm's fairy story who lost her tail and whose every step is agony. Her stomach hurts. Her legs ache, particularly the right one. Her body is full of pain. She would do almost anything to be rid of the constant pain. Is it possible this doctor could help her? She watches the tips of her black lace-up boots peeping out from beneath the hem of her white dress. She clutches her reticule.

She has taken the trouble to dress up for this doctor, though she has no desire to see him again. When she saw him briefly the first time, it was just before the dreadful visit to the lake (*she will not think about that!*) when she was fifteen. She has a vague memory of a rather small man, not as tall as her father and quite thin, with intense, dark eyes, blue-black hair, a beard, and a mustache. She remembers him saying something about calling *un chat un chat*, which he said in French, which she has learned with her French fräulein but which she had considered, even at fifteen, to belie the message.

It has just stopped raining, and the street is wet. She hangs back, dragging her right leg, taking her time, then getting into the carriage, where she sits as far as possible from her father, her gaze averted, looking out the window, in sullen silence.

The sky is dark and the cobblestones wet and slippery as the carriage moves forward, going downhill toward the

Danube Canal. The doctor's office is just around the corner and only a few minutes from their house on Lichtenstein-strasse, but she cannot walk even that far without terrible pain. She has lost her voice again, too, and in the damp air, she is afraid she may have an attack of coughing, which makes her lose her breath and terrifies her. There is nothing more terrifying than not being able to breathe. She is afraid she will die asphyxiated, gasping for breath on the street where she was born. If she has consented to see this doctor, it is because she does not want to die in that way. She concentrates on her breathing. When she swallows her throat feels tight and sore. The whole world looks dark to her, seen through a fog of pain. After a while nothing else matters much except for the pain. She wonders if life is worth living like this.

Her father is sitting next to her in the shadows and watching her with his soft, deep blue, caressing gaze. He still cannot see out of his left eye, which has a slightly milky appearance. The miraculous thing is that, on the point of losing his sight in his good eye, he regained his sight in the eye that was blind. She thinks of the expression "*in the kingdom of the blind, the one-eyed man is king.*" He has clotted, dark lashes. There is something innocent about his gaze, though she knows he is not innocent at all. *Not at all.*

He goes on talking about the doctor. "You'll find out, if you give him a chance, that he is a most unusual man. It takes some time to get used to him. He's a little shy and stiff. Not one of those superficial charmers who seduce you with a glance," he says, raising his eyebrows and glancing at her laughingly. "But I'm sure you will come to appreciate his brilliance, my dear. He has written many learned books and recently one about dreams, which you may read one day, perhaps, when you are a little older. He sees things so clearly and speaks so well, so persuasively. You must try to listen to what he has to say and follow his advice." He reaches across the carriage for her hand, squeezes her fingers. She disengages her gloved hand and gives him as sullen a look as she dares. She would like to say, "fat lot of good talking does!" She can imagine the lies he must already have told the doctor. She imagines him saying, "My daughter has a wild imagination. She has been making things up. She must be made to see reason."

He is a Jewish doctor, of course, the best kind, and has even been called a miracle worker, her father says, exaggerating, she imagines, as usual, as the carriage stops on the sloping street of the quiet and respectable, if not exactly distinguished, neighborhood, before the solid wooden door with the number 19 Berggasse. Their footsteps echoing, they go along the narrow, dark passage, which leads to the few steps on the right, up to the ground floor office with the sign on the brown door that announces, "Dr. Sigmund Freud."

III

THE DOCTOR AND
THE RELUCTANT GIRL

THE PATIENT IS LATE, HE thinks with annoyance, looking at his watch. He is afraid the father will not manage to convince the spoiled girl to come. She sounds as if she has become quite a handful. When he saw her briefly a couple of years earlier, she was not much older than his eldest girl, his sensible Mathilde, is today. He had proposed treating her then, but she had recovered sufficiently—or so he was told—and refused to return. Now, her father has insisted she do so. But will she actually turn up? Will the doting father convince his cosseted daughter to come?

They might at least have used the telephone to announce their delay. He has had that necessary apparatus, the telephone, installed in his office for several years.

He paces uneasily back and forth over the Persian carpets. He looks up at the statue of the two-faced stone Janus he bought recently, which seems to regard him with a superior snarl, and wonders if this new patient might be a mistake, but he tells himself he has little choice. He needs the florins, and the father has them.

The father has become extremely rich, whereas he, who was such a hardworking and brilliant student, has only a few patients this month, and must worry about money. This paucity of patients is a continual source of anxiety. Herr E. has finally left after five years of therapy, and his faithful elderly patient has died, which has cut off a steady source of revenue. It has been a long time since Breuer referred anyone to him. Breuer has been very good to him over the years—they even wrote a book together—and has helped him financially again and again, but the man lacks courage. In the end he had fled, grabbed his hat in a state of panic and perspiration—or so he remembers being told—and run from his neurotic patient when she announced she was bearing his child.

He is reminded of his father's story of being accosted in the street by an arrogant Christian who threw his father's splendid cap into the gutter and told him to get off the sidewalk; he had simply stepped into the road, picked up the cap, and gone on his way. Only Fliess seems to have followed in Hannibal's father's footsteps, the father who made his son swear to take revenge on the Romans. Only Fliess has had the courage of his convictions, but perhaps this is at least in part because he has the means.

He thinks of all the people he is responsible for: his six children, *his worms*, who need new shoes; his wife, who complains about his extravagance; his sister-in-law, Minna, who has come to live with them since her fiancé died of tuberculosis five years ago and who has recently had an intervention; and Marie, their devoted maid.

Having known the helplessness that comes with poverty, he continues to fear it. His uncle, Josef, he knows, was tried and convicted of selling an enormous number of counterfeit rubles in a desperate attempt to attain wealth. His father, who had turned white after this event, had never recovered completely from the implications of his brother's imprisonment. He remembers his own years of solitude and struggle, separated from his fiancée and desperately attempting to make a living. He recalls walking the streets of Vienna and staring with longing into the shop windows, going past Reitmayer and Ettlinger and the jeweler to the court, Schafransky. Since his father's death, his own position is less precarious financially as he is no longer obliged to support him as well. Since his death he has even been able to begin his collection of antiquities. He looks with some satisfaction at the Florentine copy of Michelangelo's *Dying Slave*, in his swooning stance.

He feels quite isolated within the world of medicine, even ridiculed. He remains unrecognized, passed over again and again for the professorship that would bring prestige and, above all, financial security, a position that has been accorded to people, usually Gentiles, much younger and much less accomplished than he, a position that surely he deserves. He has such a thirst for knowledge, such determination to find it, such clarity of mind, such ability to seize upon the essential and to render it understandable in crystalline prose. How his brain teems! He has missed so many opportunities for fame and advancement.

Above all he needs to document his theories with facts drawn from the lives of his patients. His critics have accused him of not giving verifiable examples to back up his theories. Perhaps this patient, if she ever arrives, will provide some.

He has left the door to his consulting room open and has become so engrossed in his thoughts that at first he does not notice the real girl standing in the doorway, trembling in her white dress like the sail of a boat in the wind. She looks younger than her age, this slip of a girl, dark haired, dewy eyed, and blooming with youth: her pale cheeks and forehead touched with a faint tinge of pink. She has a luminosity about her and despite her reluctance to enter, an unusual assurance in her stance and mien. She hesitates in his doorway in her delicate organdy dress with the green silk sash that accentuates her slender waist, an expensive dress, he thinks with a little pang of envy, the sort he cannot buy for his own three girls.

The girl stands there before him, ravishing in all her youthful splendor, her dark thick hair long on her shoulders, her broad gold bracelets glinting on her wrist.

Increasingly, his patients are from the small circle of wealthy Jewish bourgeoisie. He thinks of Anna von L., whom he saw sometimes twice a day, his prima donna, as he called her, from the wealthy Ephrussi family, who was brought to him because no one knew what to do with her, a woman of sophistication who taught him a lot in the end. This one's dress he is certain his wife would covet, though after six children in almost as many years, she no longer has as fine a waist to show it off.

The tall, handsome father stands behind the daughter like a dark shadow cast on the bright waters, his hand possessively on her white shoulder. "I leave you in very good hands, my dear," the father says in a mellifluous tone, smiling down at his daughter, and across the room at him with complicity. He does not smile back, just bows his head briefly in acknowledgment and waits for the father to leave, but the man lingers, leaning elegantly against the lintel. He wonders why he does not have the good grace to go and leave the daughter with him. Instead, he stands there smiling with all the assurance of the successful businessman he is, in his fine gray gloves, his dark suit, silk hat in hand.

He is glad he is wearing his best pinstriped trousers, a little bow tie, a new corduroy jacket with the hand stitching that he feels gives him a certain presence. Even decent clothes were a problem for him for many years. He had not known how to acquire all the necessary absurd accoutrements for his examinations: the top hat, etc., when he was obliged to present himself in formal dress.

He remembers how he kept an account, recording all his expenses, the money he spent on the two meals a day he felt he could afford—his books, and his cigars, his only extravagance for years. Sometimes, he could not afford to take a cab for his house visits. So many of his schemes, which seemed so hopeful, have come to naught. He thinks of his early lectures, his sparkling, inspired words wasted on so few attendees, and these all drummed up with difficulty; his book on aphasia, which sold only 257 copies and had to be pulped; his work on cocaine, for which Köller got all the credit, and he, only grave reproaches.

The father, he knows, has no such problems, his accounts

on the contrary always on the credit side of the ledger at the Bank Ephrussi. His wife, unlike his own, has come with a fine dowry. He pays his bills with regularity and generosity, a good bottle of cognac or even opera tickets—the doctor has seen *Don Giovanni*, one of his favorite operas, in Salzburg thanks to him—thrown in from time to time. Both the father's and the mother's family have been successful in the textile business, like many of the Bohemian Jews based in Vienna who still have wool or linen factories in the Bohemian countryside.

Indeed, he thinks, the father's childhood in a small country town must not have been very different from his own, though, unlike him, the father never showed much aptitude or interest at school, and did not attend the university.

As he stares at the father he sees tears glittering in the man's blue eyes as he looks down at his daughter.

She does not look up at her father or at him, but gazes blankly at the carpet, her long lashes lowered sullenly. What secrets does her shuttered gaze hide? What is her story? What can he do for her? What does she want of him?

He beckons for the girl to enter his office and watches the father give her a gentle push. He ushers the elegant girl in, nods to the frowning father, who looks as though he might break down and weep, and closes the door firmly on him.

"Make yourself comfortable," he says to the girl and indicates the ottoman, a gift from a grateful patient. The girl eyes it with suspicion and perches there stiffly as though sitting on eggshells, her back ramrod straight, feet planted neatly side-by-side, hands firmly clutching her reticule as though she were afraid someone might snatch it from her.

Since the girl's first visit to him, she has seen many doctors who have not been able to help her. Her behavior has become increasingly troublesome at home. She needs to understand, the father maintains, that her demands are very rude and unreasonable, going even so far as to suggest he break off his friendship with old and dear friends of the family. She, who was so angelic, who looked after him with such devotion in his various illnesses, has become sullen and bad tempered with both her parents, and her symptoms are worse, particularly the cough, the pains in her leg, the aphasia.

He stares at her hands. Gestures tell us a great deal, he has learned from his favorite writers as well as from Charcot, a *visuel* who had the nature of an artist, a man who saw, who taught him not to take anything for granted but to look and look again in order to understand. He thinks of Charcot saying, "*La théorie c'est bon, mais ça n'empêche pas d'exister.*" She has long-fingered hands with white knuckles, and the nails bitten down to the quick. She looks as if a slight breeze could unseat her and carry her off.

The doctor recalls his bashful patient, Herr E., who would blush with the desire to ravish every woman he saw, perhaps a more common feeling than is generally admitted to by those of his sex.

She seems to stare with fascination at the lithograph he brought back from his year in Paris.

"What is wrong with the girl?" she asks, gesturing toward the lithograph without looking at him.

Taken aback for a moment, he stares at the beautiful Blanche Wittman, seeing her anew through this girl's eyes: her smooth shoulders and bodice indecently exposed, leaning back into the arms of Charcot's assistant, the lucky doctor Babinski, surrounded by a group of staring men during one of Charcot's Tuesday lessons.

"Too tightly laced," he deems it expedient to reply and thinks of the talented Blanche, whom they called the "Queen of Hysterics."

When this girl finally directs her gaze toward him her eyelids seem heavy, the long, dark lashes weighing them down. Her eyes are large and wide spaced, like her father's, and lucent but sullen. He realizes with a little shock that this girl is in a rage. She gives him a blank but angry stare. He thinks of the English expression "*if looks could kill.*"

For a moment he regrets no longer being able to use hypnosis on a girl of this kind. It might be easier to get her to comply. He thinks of his early success with the mother whom he hypnotized, who could not feed her baby. He has been obliged to give it up as, unlike Charcot, he has often had difficulty putting his patients to sleep, which was perhaps a blessing in disguise, as it has forced him to come up with other, more lasting methods.

He stares back at the girl and is about to explain his new method, what Breuer's former patient has aptly dubbed "the talking cure," when she asks disconcertingly, looking around the room disdainfully, "Why do you have all these old statues?"

"The psychoanalyst," he says, drawing himself up, "like the archaeologist, must clear away layer after layer, as though digging down through a buried city, in order to reach the deepest layers of the patient's mind to discover the secrets that lie buried there." He points to the Roman statue of a child on the table by his chair and thinks of the city of Rome and how he both wants and fears to visit it. He is afraid of contracting an illness there in the summertime, which is when he is free to travel.

"How very interesting!" she says in an inimitable tone and peers at the statue, rather like a grande dame being led through a museum and glancing at the objects through a lorgnette.

For a moment he would like to give her a shake. He remembers how easily Charcot had access to Blanche Wittman's memories of a traumatic childhood through hypnosis: her childish, unprotected body sexually abused again and again. He remembers Charcot saying "*toujours la chose génitale—toujours, toujours!*" and wondering why, if the problem was always genital, no one ever mentioned it then.

Years later he will hear of the repeated amputations of Blanche's beautiful body, which left her with only one hand and arm. Her fingers, her other hand and arm, and both her legs were all removed because of the effects of radiation, the result of her work in the photography department at the Salpêtrière Hospital where she had been the star in Charcot's weekly demonstrations.

Now he says, "Our bodies are sometimes able to speak when we ourselves cannot. In a sense our stories are written on them. What I hope is to have you translate your story from the pain you feel into words."

He tells her he would like her to lie back on the couch, to relax, even to close her eyes if it helps her to concentrate, and simply to tell him what passes through her mind.

"You mean you want me to tell you everything I think?" she says, looking at him sharply, frowning, sounding and looking appalled at the thought, and for a moment, as the fine curtain lifts a little in the breeze and he hears a rush of beating wings, this young girl brings back his first love, the young Gisela Fluss, with her dark hair and the wild hare's look in her eyes. In the small, dimly lit room he suddenly sees the hills as blue as the sky, the grass quivering and billowing, and smells the sweet fragrance of the trees and the wildflowers all around her. For a brief moment he experiences a full-blown surge of adolescent lust, as he did returning to the village where he was born. It surprises and appalls him, here in his consulting room, this reawakening of a buoyant and total discovery of sexual longing which he had felt in his sixteenth year. It had made him horribly awkward, reduced him to a stammering young fool. Something not to be repeated, ever. He knows all the dangers of passion. He needs to be careful this girl does not catch him in her net.

He must get down to business fast. He commences speaking in as dry and matter-of-fact a tone as possible. He explains that it is by association, by linking one thing to the next, the present to the past, that the causes of her malady will be found. Nothing is too insignificant or too shocking to be stated aloud.

She glances at him blankly without moving, her gaze dull, her full lips slightly turned down at the corners in a proud scowl.

He thinks of the Baroness Fanny M., who could be quite surly at times and had told him to stop interrupting her with his numerous questions, a remark which as it turned out had been most helpful over time, however it might have caught him up short. His own mother, too, has that proud will of her own, even arranging to have her birthday fall on the same day as that of the Emperor Franz Joseph.

"I am not going to hurt you in any way," he reassures her. He says, "I need you simply to tell me freely and frankly what comes to mind without censoring your thoughts. I will leave the subjects entirely up to you and I will listen carefully, and unlike your family or friends, consider what you have to say as objectively as possible. I would like to hear your side of the story your father has told me."

"See if you can bring her to reason. She has an overstimulated imagination, nourished by reading unsuitable texts. She has been telling all sorts of wild tales," the father has said. He is aware that the father has an agenda that may be very different from his own, not to speak of the girl's.

"Ultimately," he says, "you are the one who must discover what it is that ails you. I am here simply to mirror your words."

"A mirror?" she says dubiously, opening her eyes wide and looking at him directly.

He thinks of the many devoted, loving women he has treated, who have long sat in attendance by sickbeds in darkened rooms, as she has. These intelligent and often courageous women, Breuer's Bertha P. among them, have taught him a lot with their vivid, frank talk. He remembers the young girl in the mountains who told him her sad tale of incest with more directness than most.

This one gazes at him with a flicker of interest in her dark eyes. "Within the confines of these walls," he says, indicating the ancient Egyptian and Roman statuettes, "we will not be bound by false prudery." One hour every day except Sunday will be reserved for their work together so that they may unravel the mystery behind her symptoms. "To quote the Greek philosopher Anaxagoras," he says, feeling the need for a little Greek, "the symptoms—the phenomena that we see—are just the visible expression of something hidden. Something is surely locked away, and together we must find the key to open the lock. To accomplish this, we will have to call *un chat un chat*," he says.

The girl says, in her dry, faint voice, "You said that before. And how long will you take to cure me?"

The doctor replies that, of course, it depends, but it might take up to a year.

She looks at him with disdain and says, "It would take you that long!"

He thinks of Goethe's lines from *Faust*: "Not art or science serve, alone; patience must in the work be shown," and ignores this and goes on with his explanation. He will ask her questions no one has probably ever asked her before and speak of subjects she may never have spoken of. "All we need is for you to follow what comes to your mind freely and frankly," he says.

She looks up at this and says with a glimmer of humor in her eyes that surprises him, "I will try, though it might be easier just to make things up. If you tell me I have to say everything I actually *think*, it will *make* me think unspeakable, rude things! Are you sure you really want to hear them? You might not *like* what I have to say. I wouldn't want to say anything that would *hurt* you."

He smiles slightly at this and thinks this girl is bolder than many her age. Was the father right in his surmise? Has she been making things up? He asks, "You like to make things up?" "Sometimes, yes. I do like to make up stories. But father is wrong. *I* know the difference between the truth and a lie. Truth is very important to me. I don't lie the way *he* does," she says firmly, narrowing her eyes at him. "Mostly it seems to me that no one actually wants you to tell the truth, though they might say they do. It is understood that I should say things that are pleasant and agreeable, things people want to hear," she says, moving slightly on the sofa, relinquishing her reticule for a moment. She picks up a plump pillow with both her hands, holds it on her lap like a puppy dog, stroking it absently, then positioning it behind her and leaning back. She picks up her reticule and places it on her lap again. "That's better," she says. "My leg doesn't hurt as much. As the day goes on the pain gets worse and worse. I don't know why."

The doctor recalls the numerous hysterical women he has treated for similar symptoms, common among women and even some men. Despite the revered Meynert's opinion and the origin of the word, the doctor, like Charcot, is certain hysteria exists in both sexes. Has he not known hysterical symptoms himself—shortness of breath, heart palpitations, angina, fainting?

He has used various methods to cure these symptoms with varying degrees of success over the years: electricity, pressure of the hands, even massage, and finally just obliging the patients to confront a shameful secret from the past, one that is so often hidden even from themselves.

He has listened for hours with patience, sympathy, and interest, and he has had the humility to learn from his mistakes. But the patients are usually scrupulously polite, overconscientious, arriving on time, often trembling, weeping, begging for his help, sometimes even falling in love with him, throwing their arms around his neck. It is true that this one is being more or less forced back to see him.

Faced by her silence, he is not quite sure what to say to her. An older or even a younger person would certainly be easier. He is not used to rebellious adolescents and feels he is not quite sure how to deal with this one. He was never a rebellious adolescent himself. He has worked so hard for so much of his life, earnestly aware of the sacrifices his family made for the adored boy, his mother's golden Siggie, given the privilege of his own *kabinett*, reading Shakespeare at eight, taking his meals alone, his sister's musical ambitions stifled so that he could study in silence with the only oil lamp, in the scant space of the exiguous apartment, then sent to the university at considerable cost, so that he could pursue his medical studies.

He has to admit the girl's concise speaking style is strangely convincing. He wonders how much her symptoms are simply inherited, how much she may be acting, how hysterical she is, after all.

Intelligent teenage girls are instinctively theatrical, often uttering sentences just to confuse people or to attract attention.

It seems difficult to distinguish the acting from reality here, despite her assurances. It will be in her dreams that he will find the truth.

"Above all, I would like to hear about your dreams," he tells her. "They will hold the secret to your symptoms." In the dream, he explains, it is as though the sentinel, the night watchman of our conscious thoughts, can be evaded, and the hidden desires can emerge.

"I know you are interested in dreams. I am too, though I don't always remember mine. My father told me you have written a book about them," she says with a shrewd look in her dark eyes, which again surprises him. His patients rarely bring up his writings.

He thinks of his new book on dream interpretation, which he had expected would bring him instant renown but has only brought a few bad and even malicious reviews. He wrote to Fliess, wondering if there would, someday, be a plaque on the place where the "model dream" had come to him, announcing that this was the house where the mystery of dreams was revealed to Dr. Sigmund Freud. What folly!

He glances at the portrait of the handsome, bearded Fleischl that he has hung in an oval frame on the wall, that brilliant man, whom he admired so much. What a terrible tragedy! Suddenly he remembers Fleischl's colorful parrot, wings spread, which he adored, and how he would talk to him. He will always regret bitterly the role he played in his death. He had been so hopeful that he could cure him of his morphine addiction with cocaine.

"It is through your own words that we will discover the

cure for what has troubled you for such a long time now, your *tussis nervosa*, gastric pains, ambulatory difficulty, the loss of voice," he says.

She says she hopes he can cure her fast, as she is in pain, but she continues to sit with her head slightly lowered, her petulant bottom lip protruding, her gaze on her lap. From time to time she impatiently throws a rebellious lock of hair behind her neck. He can see that she is not looking at him. Is she even listening to him? She seems to have little curiosity about or faith in the doctor who is supposed to treat her. He notices the shape of her ears beneath her small black hat, curiously shaped ones. He adds, a little sternly now—her continued sullen silence, the rigidity of her pose, her recalcitrance are beginning to annoy him—that her father is very worried about her. She stares back sullenly at him, her childish cheeks reddening.

She admits, "I can be terrible sometimes, it is true, because if I want something and I can't get it, then I am after it regardless of whether my parents like it or not," and she stares at him rudely.

He has confronted rude patients before. He thinks of the elderly woman all dressed in black who would receive him with an ivory crucifix clutched in her hand as though he were the Evil One, yet he had managed to ferret out her secrets.

"You have frightened your parents, you must be aware. Your father was particularly worried by your moment of complete unconsciousness after a quarrel with him, when you fell to the floor onto your face in the red-tiled corridor leading to the kitchen, he said. What was all that about?"

She replies, "I don't remember anything about that except finding myself on the floor."

"And the suicide note you left in your desk that upset them terribly?" he says, remembering the scream of the maid who had watched as young Pauline S., the wife of his best childhood friend, had thrown herself over the balustrade of his building in her elegant clothes.

"How on earth did they find the letter? It was shut up in my desk. Mother must have been snooping, as usual! Once, she found my imaginary diary and read it and thought that was all true!" She suddenly finds her voice, albeit a hoarse whisper, fueled by her rage, no doubt.

"We will find out why you are so unhappy, why you are suffering," he continues, trying to speak gently but firmly.

She gives him another sullen look. "You would be unhappy too, if you had to spend your days sorting out pieces of string too short to use," she says.

"I beg your pardon?" he asks.

"That's the sort of task my mother gives me—useless things. She's preoccupied with dust! The earth could crumble, and she'd still be dusting!" she spits out with disgust. "My father is a man of considerable means, as you undoubtedly know, so we have many servants, but my mother spends her time this way! The maids follow in her wake." She explains that her mother constantly hovers over the housemaids. She breaks off and looks at him with her angry stare.

"But you must know all about that, about Mother and about Father, don't you? You probably know more than I do! He's made me come to see you to persuade me to be more reasonable, hasn't he, which actually means more willing to do what *he* wants me to do?" she says, coughing and sputtering over her sentences, bending forward and putting her hands on her thighs.

"I'm not here to persuade you to do anything," he says firmly, thinking though that this girl is not far from the mark. On an impulse he says, "Your father *has* told me something about the problem, as he sees it, but I would like to hear about it from you, in order to form my own opinion. You, after all, are the only one who can help us find the truth." Recalling that the father has described the girl as unusually well read and intelligent, he quotes from his beloved Goethe, "The first and last thing required of genius is love of truth."

Suddenly the girl looks at him with a glimmer of something he takes for hope, sighs, and lies back down on his couch. He watches her breast heave with emotion, and she attempts to catch her rapid breath, her hands now relinquishing her reticule and fluttering like trapped butterflies to smooth her white organdy skirt.

IV

THE SECOND VISIT

SHE KNOWS HE IS WAITING for her to speak. She feels his impatience behind her head. This time he sits in a chair slightly at an angle to the sofa and behind her, so that she cannot see his face. She feels he is hiding back there, eavesdropping on a private conversation she is expected to produce, or as though he were playing hide-and-seek as she did with her brother in the nursery as small children, hiding from each other in the shadowy corners of the big room.

Yet what can she safely say? What stories can she tell to placate and satisfy this man, these men? What version of the truth will please them? Which of her words could actually help with her pain? What does this man want her to say?

He has asked her to tell him about her life, the history of her illnesses, when all these various troubles began. As if she could possibly do such a thing, even if she wanted to!

She says, "I only remember unimportant bits and pieces of my life. I don't really know where to begin. I had the usual childhood illnesses, like everyone else. Really my whole life seems very ordinary to me. I am an ordinary girl, except for my recent illness, the pains in my legs, the trouble with my voice, my breathing."

Her voice, which will sometimes disappear for as long as two weeks, has returned now. She is able to speak clearly, though her cough, which the doctor calls *tussis nervosa*, comes and goes and makes her feel she will lose her breath. The pains in her legs and the right side of her stomach come and go mysteriously, too. For the moment she feels no pain at all in her legs stretched out before her.

"So?" the doctor says clearing his throat as though *he* were about to speak. An impatient man. Perhaps he wants to put her in the book he is working on now. She knows he has written several, and most probably about his patients, though she has not read any of them. Perhaps she should read the latest one on dreams. She is interested in them herself.

She would like to tell the doctor that what she sees in her mind at the moment as in a dream are odd things bobbing up on the surface of a rough sea, as they do after a shipwreck: all the flotsam and jetsam, the detritus of her life, thrown up onto the surface of dark waters. She hears shutters banging, the sudden clatter of footsteps on the stairs, she sees the deep blue water of the lake glinting, the brilliant light like knives; she sees herself running along the edge of the lake; she smells smoke. Is this smoke in this place or her past?

She sees some things so clearly, others not at all. Her whole life seems a jumble of moments of panic, situations which seemed so dangerous or embarrassing, so many humiliations. She sees danger and shame everywhere. She is so afraid of making a fool of herself. Her life does not seem a continuous stream, but rather a series of separate moments, photographs in someone else's album. It is quite different from the suspenseful story, one thing causing the other to happen, which she has invented, writing about the engineering student she likes in her imaginary diary she now keeps hidden in a locked drawer.

So she remains silent, staring at the oval portrait on the wall of a bearded man, wondering who he is.

Even the doctor himself, whom she remembers from her brief visit two years ago, seems different, as if *he* were someone else. She remembers him as somewhat thinner, smaller, older, and wearing glasses. Instead, when she entered the room this afternoon, she thought he looked slightly plump, his nose shiny. He seemed rather cheerful, greeting her heartily, a man pleased with himself, or pleased with her appearance in his consulting rooms, an optimistic, perhaps even deluded man, telling her he can cure her horrid pains with words. He seems to her a typical Jewish petit bourgeois, a shopkeeper or even a dressed-up peddler, a very ordinary potentate. How could such a boring, middle-aged man, with his silly pinstriped pants and his mournful bow tie and the hand-stitching on his corduroy jacket, understand the strange story she has to tell? She hardly believes it herself. And in the end does this story have anything to do with her body, her aching limbs, her breath? How can talking make pain go away? Is the body so intimately connected with the mind? She does remember how, when she left her home for some days, she had become terribly constipated, unable to use the *klo*.

"Start away!" the doctor says, eager to earn his fee, she imagines. Her father is doubtless paying him well.

"When I was very young," she tells him, speaking clearly, her voice coming to her almost as though it belongs to someone else, telling someone else's story, "I felt much more extraordinary because everyone told me how clever I was, how quickly and early I had learned to read and write. Everyone said I was such a precocious child. I learned languages and the piano fast. I loved music—I still do. I was even good with numbers and liked to play number games."

"Numbers?" he says.

Her throat tickles. She must not start coughing, because once she starts, she cannot stop. She tries to relax as he told her to do but she feels her throat contract. She swallows. Lying on his couch for the second time, her stomach cramps, and she is afraid she might have to go to the *klo*. It is a perpetual worry in here. The first time she had to get up and go in the middle of the session, but when she got there nothing happened.

She remembers how another dreadful doctor had once made her take off her underwear and lie flat on her stomach when she was suffering from severe constipation. He had covered her back with only a towel and she had had to lie there disgracefully with her bottom stuck up in the air. Then he had reached up and put an electrode directly into what she thinks of as her most private part. With the force of the electricity there had been immediate and explosive results. She will never forget the shame of it, the awful, humiliating shame. She had wanted to die.

Now, recalling it, she has a pain down her right leg, and

she feels nauseated. The office smells of cigar smoke, she realizes, which is what is making her feel nauseated, though the window is open on this sunny fall afternoon.

She has always hated the smell of smoke and has never allowed anyone, even her father, to smoke in her own room. This doctor, like her brother and her father and his friend Herr Z., she divines, must be a smoker. She wonders if the doctor smokes the same kind of cigars as her father, which, he has told her, old Emperor Franz Joseph smokes, too. The smell is the same.

"Yes? You were a precocious child?" he says.

"I was a wild girl in those early days, free and pleased with myself," she tells him, smiling at the memory, seeing herself running fast, laughing in the woods that were close to their home, teasing her nursemaid, going through light and shade, running away from the poor, stout, breathless woman in her white cap and apron. She had even tormented her poor brother, touching his bed when he didn't want her to. "Please don't touch my bed," he would say miserably, and she would do it again with the tip of her finger just to torment him.

As she lies there a memory comes to her unbidden, and she finds herself telling the doctor: "Sometimes I was even cruel. I remember making a ring with some other girls—it was at my cousin's house, I think, at a birthday party, holding hands and circling a poor girl, a foreigner who came from England. We taunted her, telling her she had killed Joan of Arc. 'You killed Joan of Arc!' we shouted at her. I suppose we must have learned about it in some history lesson as being the fault of the English.

"In those days I didn't have any trouble with my voice or my bowels. The whole world seemed a brighter place, lit up, sunny, and clear. I felt so clever. Everything came easily to me. Sometimes I would even sign my letters 'from an undiscovered genius,'" she says and giggles at the thought. "I was not quite sure whether I would be a great writer or a great musician, but something great, I was certain. I knew I couldn't be a painter as I was no good at that, though I do love to look at paintings. There *were* famous women writers, were there not, like the English writers Charlotte Brontë and Jane Austen, but the only great women musicians I could think of were sisters or wives: Mozart's sister and Schumann's wife, Clara. I wonder if I'll be known only as Otto's sister?" she asks the doctor and giggles.

The doctor does not giggle. He says nothing to all of this. He probably thinks she is far from a genius. He probably thinks there is no such thing as a girl genius, or certainly no girl who needs to tell her story to the world. Yet how important it seems to her to record what she imagines and feels, to share it with someone even if it is only her secret diary.

She hears nothing but the ticking of the clock, the occasional crackle of the fire that burns in the tiled stove, and the muffled sounds from the courtyard, the voice of a servant girl shouting out something.

"A wild girl? In what way?" the doctor asks eventually.

She tries to go on with her tale, her cough interrupting her words: "I felt I was just as clever as my brilliant brother— though perhaps he has a better memory than I do. He can quote endlessly from books. Did you know he wrote a play about Napoléon when he was just nine? Still I felt that there was little he could do better than I could, and certain things I understood much better than he did."

The doctor does not show much interest or comment on her brother. Many years later, when Otto has indeed become famous, a charismatic social leader, she will learn that the doctor has advised him not to try and make people happy, because that is not what they really want.

Still she continues, "We were inseparable. I loved—still love him so much, more than my life. One of my earliest memories is of sitting very close to him with my arm around his neck and pulling on his earlobe and sucking my thumb. We were sitting up in the bay window in the nursery, and it was almost as if he were part of me, and I were part of him," she says, so sad in the silence of this dim room that what she remembers is no longer the case—that she is now here alone with this silent, distant man.

What *is* the doctor doing back there? What is he thinking? She doesn't hear him writing down her words or even moving. Could he have passed out, fainted, as she has done before? Is he dead? She doesn't dare look back. She is like Orpheus in the underworld, unable to look back or the doctor will disappear. She doesn't want him to disappear.

Or perhaps he is actually snoozing after a heavy luncheon, as her father does sometimes in his study. Has he drunk a few beers or glasses of wine? He might, after all, be a drinker or even take drugs. Who knows? He sports too neat a waistcoat, too shiny a gold fob watch, and too neatly clipped a beard and mustache. He probably visits a barber daily and goes for his stroll on the Ringstrasse, marching along doggedly with a distracted gaze, like all the good bourgeois of Vienna: the very earnest sort of person who is trying too hard. He is not as elegant, or playful, or aristocratic as her auburn-haired, blue-eyed father, or nearly as handsome, though the doctor does have bright eyes that seem to see her. Nor does he have any of her father's charm, but perhaps that is just as well. He is not an ugly man, though quite old, of course, as old as her father, as old as Herr Z.

She speaks into the silence, "In the beginning, I could keep up with my brother, as he shared many of the books he read at the *Gymnasium*, but now since he has continued with his studies at the university, where I am not allowed to go, he has passed me by. He is interested in things in the wider world. He worries so about the poor weavers who work in such difficult conditions, for such long hours, and for so little money in Father's factories in Bohemia. Like my uncle, Karl, he is always talking about politics, about how he wishes to do something useful for his fellow man.

"But what possibilities do I have to help my fellow man or even myself, for that matter? And though he always *says* he loves me, and I know he does, what has my brother ever done for *me* in reality? He almost always takes Mother's side in the end," she says and clenches her fists against the rug on the couch.

She runs her fingers over the silky soft Persian rug which covers the couch where she lies, wondering why something that belongs on the floor should have been put on a couch.

She traces the zigzag of the pattern of white birds and the

strange winged creatures with fanned tails. She is in a cocoon spun of silken threads by skilled hands. The doctor and her father are trying to lull her into a false sense of security with all this false luxury, this appearance of calm, the shutters drawn on the afternoon sun, the inner courtyard sounds muffled by thick walls, the silky carpet to caress her body, so that she will tell them her secrets, but she knows she is in danger in this place.

She has been carried off by her father into this dim, silent, shadowy room, an Aladdin's cave or perhaps even the lion's den, and if she doesn't speak, if she doesn't find the right words, like Scheherazade she will be put to death. This doctor trades in dangerous secrets in this small dark room, she suspects. What will he do with hers should she be so foolish as to share them with him?

From the doctor's silence, she deduces he is not particularly interested in her studies or lack thereof, nor the injustice of her brother being able to study when she cannot.

"I have tried to learn what he was learning by reading on my own or with the fräulein and going to visit museums. Like you, I am interested in art. I have been to the Secessionist show several times."

She wonders whether the doctor has so many art objects in his cluttered consulting rooms because he is afraid of emptiness, of space, of silence. What did the art teacher in the evening class call that? Something like *horror vacui*?

She stares at all the ancient figurines, deities and seers perhaps, from different places and ages that the doctor has collected. She doesn't feel his answer to her question about them explained anything. She likes the little statue of a child, perhaps Roman, who has an old face, because it looks the way she feels, an adolescent who is already old. But he says nothing about that so she goes on, still bent on impressing him with what she considers her valiant efforts to learn.

"I love listening to music. I play the piano every afternoon and have piano lessons twice a week. We often go to concerts and operas. Father took us to see *Die Fledermaus* at the Hofoper and also *The Geisha* recently, which I liked so much. I even managed to persuade Father to let me attend night classes for women, but they don't teach the same things. It is a losing battle."

He makes no comments on her efforts to become cultured, to shine in some intellectual way, which is so important to her. He does not even make any sympathetic noises, nor does he proffer any words of advice or encouragement, as her brother, at least, does. This is not the story he wants her to tell, she understands.

Probably he thinks women's education a waste of time, as most men his age do. Probably he thinks women belong in the home with their children. Only the young engineer she has met—such an elegant young man, in his gray cloak and butterfly-shaped tie, with his long fine fingers, has been sympathetic to her complaints, has even met her at the museum, and has listened with interest to her comments on the paintings.

So she returns to the subject of her illness, which is, after all, why she is here and which does seem to interest the doctor.

"I don't remember when it all began. Otto, my brother, always got the illnesses first."

"How much older is he than you?" the doctor now asks.

"Eighteen months older," she replies and tells him her brother always had a more mild case, the lucky thing, and then, of course, he would pass the disease on to her. "I would always be much more severely ill than he was," she says, aware of the bitterness in her voice.

She thinks how everyone in her family gets things from each other. The men, if she has understood rightly, mostly passing on their illnesses to the women. No wonder women prefer not to give men what they demand in the dark; no wonder her mother prefers to polish the furniture, to wash, to dust, to clean. Her father has passed on his shameful illness to her mother, she knows. And what of her own body's leaking, which it does so embarrassingly, staining her undergarments so that she scrubs them at night herself to keep the maids from seeing the shameful yellow stain? But how could she speak of that?

Instead, at his urging, she says it was when she was eight that things changed for her. She started getting the cough then, and somewhat later, around twelve, the awful migraines and the constipation, the pains in the stomach and legs a little later. The migraines went away, but she still gets the cough, which frightens her and makes her feel she might suffocate.

"The doctors all did such ghastly things to me to get rid of it, giving me electric shocks all over, even in the most embarrassing places, and thrusting things down my throat, so that I felt I would choke. Sometimes I passed out with the pain and the fear, or I vomited. They wrapped me in cold sheets, sprayed my body with hard, cold showers, and almost drowned me in cold baths. They tortured me! Really they did!" she says and sits up and waves her hands around, her bracelets chinking, exaggerating a bit for effect.

Some of these remedies were not quite as unpleasant as she has made out. Sometimes the warm baths and the massages had been quite pleasant and relaxing and made her feel a bit better.

"But really, in my opinion," she says grandly, feeling quite clever and grown up to have thought of it, "Modern doctors are not much better than the fake one I read about in Molière." She says the title, showing off her good French accent, *Le Malade imaginaire*.

"You read that?" the doctor says, sounding quite shocked.

"Yes, I did, with the French fräulein, and we laughed a lot. She introduced me to all sorts of things," she tells him with a certain pride, giggling a little, thinking of the girl in the play, who like her has lost her voice, and of the pretend doctor who says he needs to give an enema to the wet nurse, whom he thinks of as a tasty crumpet, only to have Geronte ask why she needs to be irrigated if nothing has blocked her.

"And your fräulein considered this appropriate reading for a young girl? What were you, fifteen or so?" the doctor asks, sounding really rather prudish. Could he actually be a prudish man under all this exterior of frank talk and spilled secrets?

"Well, I thought you said we should call a *chat un chat*," she cannot help responding, feeling rather pleased with herself and spreading her pretty organdy skirt with the fine embroidery across his couch, playing with her glossy ringlets. Perhaps this will be more entertaining than she thought. Perhaps he is not all that brilliant, after all, if he needs to have things both ways.

"Doctors have done me more harm than good," she tells him rather smugly, folding her arms and turning up her toes in her soft, shiny leather boots, which fit her like gloves, adding that they seem to be mostly a band of quacks. Finally, she refused to see any more of them.

"But in my case your father insisted?" the doctor asks.

"Yes, because you had helped him when he was so ill."

The doctor gives a sort of little snort which might be either a chuckle or a sound of disapproval; she's not sure. Perhaps he agrees with her about the other doctors, or perhaps he, too, has used electricity or who knows what drastic methods himself.

She fears that if she talks about her cough, it will start up again, and she will not be able to breathe, or perhaps she will lose her voice completely. So she simply changes the subject.

V

HER FATHER'S ILLNESS

THE DOCTOR TOLD HER ON the first visit that she could talk about anything she wanted to, and that he wished to hear her side of the story, so this time she decides to speak of her father rather than her intellectual prowess, which does not seem to have impressed him particularly. She wants the doctor to know what an exceptionally good, loving daughter she has been, until it became impossible to continue.

She says that she had always loved her father. "Unlike the way I felt about Mother, the way I felt about Father seemed as natural, as much a part of me as the beating of my heart," she says, crossing her hands and laying them flat against her chest. She is not quite sure where her heart is. She was so afraid he might die.

"We had to move to Meran in the South Tyrol. It was such a long way from Vienna—more than two hundred miles," she tells the doctor, though he probably knows. "Everyone told me how lucky I was to go there, how beautiful it was with the blue mountains and the rushing river and the flowers. You must know the place—it's so well known. Perhaps you have visited it with your family?" she asks.

The doctor says nothing in response, but her father will tell her later that both the doctor's wife and his sister-in-law have visited the spas in the town, and much later, of course, more than seven years later, she will hear that the doctor has sent his own eldest daughter, Mathilde, there. Now he only tells her to go on with her account.

"I wish we had never gone there."

"And why is that?"

"If we had never had to move there then nothing bad would have happened. We would never have met the Z.'s, Father and Mother's friends, such bad people whom I *hate! Hate!*"

"The Z.'s? Bad people? And why do you hate these people?" he asks.

"I don't want to talk about them," she says and goes on about leaving her home.

"It was all so awful from the start: the move from our big house in Vienna was so sad. I remember standing alone in the empty nursery with its pale-green walls and only the three beds for me, my brother, and the nursemaid, and the three bedside tables with the china chamber pots beneath them still remaining. I was looking around for my lost doll."

"A doll?" the doctor asks.

"I still have her—a lucky rag doll with a black face, you know, one my great-uncle brought back from a trip to New Orleans—Brigit, I call her. She still lies on my pillow and protects me, in her old threadbare dress, from harm, or so I imagine.

"Do you believe in magic, Doctor? Do you think all these old statues will protect you?" she asks, pushes her hair back from her face, and wonders if some of the little statues are fakes. It would be easy to fake things of that kind, surely. She wonders if the doctor paid a lot of money for them.

But he doesn't talk about magic or even money, just tells her to go on with her story, the move to Meran.

"I was sucking my thumb—I was a thumb sucker and must have been seven or eight—but I can still see myself standing at the door of the nursery in a red smocked dress and pigtails, breathless, and hear Mother's voice calling me to hurry up and come along—when the breeze lifted the curtain and I spotted my lucky doll, Brigit, on the windowsill of the big bay window. I ran across the room to pick her up, wiping away tears. My poor brother was even sadder than I was to have to leave the house and particularly the two big dogs. He wept so bitterly.

"Then I had to go and say good-bye to my cousins and my dearest Aunt Malvine, who was so often ill. I remember kissing my three cousins, three girls, who lived nearby, embracing them standing there so solemnly in their pinafores and plaits in the dark hallway of their house, as though I were the one who was dying. I remember the umbrella stand with the canes with funny handles, and the portrait of some old man looking down at me disapprovingly, and the narrow stairs that I ran up to find my aunt who lay on her daybed, looking so pale, with such dark rings under her eyes, lying there on her soft white pillows."

"This is your father's sister?" the doctor asks.

"Yes. You see I have always felt so much closer to my father's side of the family. I take after them in every way. I look much more like them physically than I do like Mother and her family, who are small and plump and have fine fair hair. We are all tall and have thick dark hair, though father has red in his hair, and none of us are good eaters. We are slender, and if I say so myself, handsome, and much more intelligent than Mother's family—or anyway Father certainly is, and I'm afraid many of us are ill—my uncle, too, Father's brother is often ill—perhaps it runs in the family—but I was particularly fond of my Aunt Malvine, Father's sister.

"That day I remember how she stretched her arms out to me and said, 'Come and kiss me, darling child,' and I ran to her. When she reached across and picked me up and held me tightly in her thin arms, I could feel her ribs and smell the odor of sickness on her breath. I so hated to leave her and to know I would never be able to go down the road with my nursemaid to visit her in the afternoons. Unlike Mother, and though she was so ill, she would always find time to read to me or answer my questions, or play imaginary games. She let me play with her jewelry and her cosmetics: her creams and lotions—I would put them all over my face, and heap her jewelry around my neck and wrists, sitting at her dressing table.

"I was so afraid that if I left her she would die, which was what happened, of course. I was right. She was such an unhappy lady—her marriage was not a happy one, so she was often alone, and she died very young.

"There has been so much illness in my family, in my life,"

she tells the doctor. "Death always seems so close to us, hovering, right here," and she puts her hands to her chest and coughs, "with my dearest aunt, my father, with his bad lungs, his tuberculosis, his blind eyes, even Mother often, too, and then Frau Z., but I don't want to talk about *her.*"

She remembers arriving in Meran and being carried half-asleep into the carriage from the station, dark clouds passing across the sky, and the mountains seeming to loom over her, dark and frightening, and the wild sound of the rushing water.

"They told me the air up there was clearer, purer, and would be good for Father's bad lungs, but I felt I could hardly breathe," she says and feels again that breathlessness in this small dark room. "I wondered how anything could flourish up there: flowers or trees. It seemed so airless and quiet." The cluttered space in the room, too, is silent, apart from the sounds from the courtyard: the raucous cry of a crow. The ceiling seems low and the clutter makes her feel hemmed in as the mountains had done.

But she tries to go on with her tale at his urging: "The air was too thin, and all the lights faintly glimmering in the small windows looked like trapped stars. It seemed such a grim place to me from the start, and I began coughing immediately as we entered the dark rooms of the old hotel with all the heavy furniture, the curtains drawn, the doilies on the arms of the heavy chairs with claws for feet, the big fires blazing in the fireplaces, though it seemed so warm to me.

"I was so frightened by the strange medicinal smells and the sight of so many sick people, many of them elderly, being pushed around in wicker bath chairs with blankets over their knees or walking around with the help of canes."

She sat staring in silence through what seemed to her endless dull meals—she ate now with her parents in the silent, vast dining rooms of the hotel, the staff coming and going noiselessly in soft shoes and white gloves, serving course after course, all in rich sauces she didn't like. She listened to the scrape of silver on porcelain, the murmur of soft voices. There were so few children her age, and those who were there, she did not know. Some of them were foreigners: Russians, Poles—people came from all over, her father told her, because of the mild climate and the curative powers of the grapes and whey. Many spoke in strange tongues. There was no one there she loved, except for her father and her brother, but he was soon sent away to school and her father had to lie in a dark room. She was bored and lonely. She was taught at home by the fancy new fräulein, who was engaged for her, though there was a Catholic school for girls, run by the nuns.

"Father didn't want me to go there, because he said they would want me to convert, so that I wouldn't be damned and have to go to hell and be consumed eternally in the fire," she says. Catholics always did, according to her father, as they thought you went to hell and were eternally burned in the fire if you were a Jew or even a Protestant and did not believe in their Savior, which always seemed odd to her as the Savior, Jesus of Nazareth, was himself, after all, a Jew and presumably was not consumed in any fire.

She met no one outside the house that they moved to

eventually, spending all her free time in the dark room beside her father, whom she loved so much and whose illness worried her terribly. She shared a nursery with her brother and the fräulein for a while, but mostly she was in her father's dark, close room. The worst moments were when he lay very still on his bed, helpless—he could hardly move his limbs at all—and seemed to have lost his mind.

"You must know how ill father has been on and off, ever since I was six years old. He often called on me to nurse him, and I went gladly, hoping to help him in some way. When he had to lie flat on his back in the dark after the operation on his one good eye, I sat beside him and whispered to him. I recited his favorite poems. *Kennst du das Land, wo die Zitronen bluehn? Im dunklen Laub die Gold-Orangen glühn, Ein sanfter Wind vom blauen Himmel whet, Die Myrte still und hoch der Lorbeen steht.*" As she recites the lovely words by Goethe, lying on the doctor's soft carpet, her voice trembles with emotion, tears coming into her eyes as she remembers those moments in the half dark with the odors of illness in the airless room, her father's hand in hers, the fear that he would be completely blind and unable to see her or anything else, that they would all be left without any means of making a living.

She knows at the same time she is showing off a bit, but she expects the doctor to be swept away by her excellent recitation, her devotion, the pathos of the situation, as people usually are.

She waits for him to praise her good memory, her voice, her taste, or at least her devotion, but again he disappoints her, remaining silent, apparently unmoved. She continues, telling him, "Father said *I* was the only one who could comfort him, who understood him. Only *I* knew what he wanted, just from the pressure of his hand on mine. I would gladly have given my life for him," she says, her voice shaking a little dramatically, recalling at the same time things whispered, things overheard about his other ailments, shameful ones that come from loose living. She says, "I overheard my great-aunt—an elderly lady who came to visit from Bohemia—say something to Mother about his 'other' illness, how it came from what my aunt called 'loose living.' Was that so, Doctor?" She waits to see if he will say something about that, which he must know about and perhaps confirm.

"I remember how very ill he was," the doctor says with sympathy in his voice.

She goes on speaking clearly now without coughing. Her breath comes easily. She finds herself encouraged to speak to this doctor who listens so carefully. Though she cannot see his face, she can almost feel his dark eyes gazing at her, as though she were something he needed, water or air, a source of life. No one has ever listened to her this carefully, not even her father when she was very young. It is as if each of her words has echoes and tells the doctor many things, a whole story which he is composing. Though he does not write them down, he seems to remember exactly what she has said from day to day.

"I can still see the darkened, hushed room"—not really so unlike the silent room where she now lies herself, she thinks—"the nurse in her stiff cap, which perched on the top of her head like a little boat, who was called in to help with

Father. I can still hear the rustle of her starched uniform and smell the carbolic acid. I remember how Father became red in the face and shouted out angrily at me when he saw me coming into the doorway, taking me for someone else, a stranger, or anyway, someone frightening, and the nurse had come rushing at me like a white wave to push me out of the room. It was so awful," she says. "It made me afraid I was not myself at all, if my father couldn't recognize me."

"It was during this illness that I first met your father, who came to consult with me in Vienna," the doctor says.

"It was his friend, Herr Z., who brought him to you, was it not?" she asks, suddenly remembering her father telling her that this was how he first met the doctor.

"Yes," the doctor admits. "That is how your father first came to me."

"Because Herr Z., too, was one of your patients?" she asks.

But the doctor says only, "I was able to relieve your father of his serious symptoms, and I expect to be able to do that for you, too."

Suddenly she doubts him entirely. She thinks now how they are all connected, these three false, middle-aged men: her father, Philipp, who has brought her to the doctor to get her to do what he wishes; Herr Z., Hans, who has intense dark eyes like the doctor, and has his own plans for her; and this doctor, whose name is Sigmund, she has read in the dream book that she found on her father's desk, who wants to use her deepest secrets for his own means, no doubt. The three of them even smell of the same foul smoke, like three devils, like three fallen angels in the flames of hell in the poem by Milton, which she has read with her fräulein. They can pretend, but they cannot disguise their evil smell.

She remembers Herr Z. rolling a cigarette for her beside the lake. "Have you ever tried one of these?" he had asked her in the light and shadow of the trembling leaves, the water of Lago di Garda glinting.

NOVEMBER 1900

———

V I

MEN AND WOMEN

HE SITS AT HIS DESK and waits impatiently for the girl to arrive. He is glad to have this new case, this young girl, however difficult she might be. Yesterday, she went on at length and quite monotonously about her father. He wants to explain the secondary benefits of illness. It is important she understand how she is using her illness to get her father's attention. She complains that her father has sent her to him to get her to do what he wishes, but behind that lies her own wish to get her father to do what *she* wishes. The doting father seems willing to do almost anything for her, including paying for a session that she does not attend. Once again the rude girl is very late.

He looks at the clock and decides to distract himself by writing to his friend Fliess about this new case. He writes a few words and then puts down his pen and runs his hand over the ring of bronze statuettes and terra-cotta figurines. He moves them as he once did his toy soldiers when he was a child. He remembers sticking labels on the flat of their backs with Napoléon's marshals' names on them. He is on a quest for origins: of this new patient's illness, of her early memories, her dreams, of his own symptoms, of his faults and failures. Above all he desires renown, which will come surely from finding the origins of these illnesses of the mind.

He stares at the figurines, which he thinks of as his old and grubby gods and uses as weights for his papers and for his fleeting and flickering ideas, trying to pin them down, to catch them in his net. He particularly likes the Egyptian ones he has been able to acquire quite cheaply and which suggest the beginnings of civilization.

He tries to write a few words to his friend but is overcome by a sensation of dizziness. Like his young patient he often faints. He gets up and pours himself a glass of water from the glass pitcher on the table by the window.

His children all have colds and sore throats and his youngest boy, Ernst, an elevated temperature, which worries him. Certainly his children have his attention when they are ill. Above all he craves a cigar. He is trying once again to follow Fliess's prescription, no doubt a wise one, not to smoke. He finds it impossible, harder even than giving up cocaine, which he was taking in ever larger quantities and distributing to his fiancée and friends. When he tries to stop the cigars, he feels an arrhythmia, a breathlessness, and a burning in his chest. The smoking calms him, the sucking has a soothing effect, enables him to work the ten hours a day it takes him to earn the one hundred florins he and his family need.

Also, he has not received a response from Fliess for several days, which makes him feel something close to panic. "Why do you not write to me? And where is my new patient?" he says aloud. He is often in a mental conversation with Fliess, running his ideas by him, trying to see them as his Other would do. How hard it is to live alone in the solitude and silence of this room.

He remembers how he longed for letters from his fiancée when they were separated, and if Martha did not write for a day or two, how desperate he was. His life seemed to hang on a thread—a letter from his beloved. It has not changed that much, he feels, though the letter writer has. Since their last meeting, Fliess does not answer his letters as rapidly as he would like, and again he feels abandoned, perhaps, as he did when his mother went away to have a baby, following the imprisonment of his nursemaid, and he feared she, too, might be locked away. Like his dreams, his feelings stand on two legs: one in the present and one in the past. One echoes the other.

He is afraid his friend is withdrawing from him. Will they ever have another "congress," he wonders, after the last one in August at Lake Achensee, when they quarreled bitterly over who had come up first with the idea of bisexuality in human beings and its role in the neuroses. He can see them both clearly walking along the edge of the lake arguing fiercely, waving their hands in the air, rather like an old married couple.

Not having heard from Fliess for several days and his patient's tardiness—has she decided already to abandon the treatment?—have brought on a feeling of breathlessness. His heart flutters, and he cannot help thinking again of his young patient's words about the presence of death in her family. Without his friend's approval of his work and the promise of his company in the future, life seems without purpose. How will he write anything new if he cannot share it as he did the dream book, chapter by chapter, listening to his suggestions and taking them seriously? And without his writing, how can he continue to live? Without his friend's approval, how can he bear the constant criticism of the medical world around him? How viciously they have attacked him for pointing out what is obvious! Even Krafft-Ebing had called his lecture on the origin of hysteria—admittedly a theory he has revised—a scientific fairy tale. How that had stung! In the shadows of the late afternoon, looking at the clock, his heart beating irregularly, he feels he is only good at heart-misery.

He has already, inexplicably, lost two good friends: first the charming and successful Breuer, a man who radiated optimism and who sincerely sought to do good, and now, perhaps, his adored Fliess. It is too hard to work alone. He crumples up the piece of paper before him. He is determined that he will not write to him and complain about this silence—he will not beg.

When he finally hears the patient's footsteps in his waiting room, his heart beats hard. He is a hunter stalking his prey. He is an adventurer, a conquistador, Pisarro, a searcher of gold! He is hunting down the truth of the heart, and this girl must be made to give it to him, whether she wishes to or not.

But when the girl enters his room, her skin glowing, her

perfume like a breath of sweet air, her thick dark hair partly pinned back and partly free around her shoulders, her "Good day" clear, he loses all his confidence. What does she really want of him, coming in, leaning on her maid's arm? She looks better today, unexpectedly, and she does not cough as she enters the room, though she does still look rather pale and shaky in her white dress.

He watches her walk across the room to his couch and waits for her to continue her story, but when she finally lies down on his couch in her finery—she seems to be wearing another new and splendid dress—sighing profoundly and waving her hands around dramatically, her gold bracelets clinking, it is in stubborn silence.

"Well?" he says. "You were telling me about your father's illness, the deaths in your family, and how that made you feel." She waves her hands, sighs again, and tells him that she cannot think of how to go on. He would like to tell her she is wasting his time and her father's money.

He stares at the dark Etruscan funerary urn he has placed in a corner of the room and thinks of the girl's words about death and illness in her family, the beloved aunt who was so important to her, and about his own dead father. He continues to miss *him* more than he ever realized he would. He had not been aware how important the man was in his life. During his life his father had often made him think of Dickens's Micawber, a tragicomical figure, someone who always believed something would turn up. He had borrowed, begged, and who knows, perhaps even stolen so that his boy could study.

Something he had forgotten comes to him: riding on the train once, sitting opposite his father in the window seat and watching him fall asleep with the sun on his face, his mouth slightly open, a thread of saliva on his chin. He remembers staring at his smooth, innocent sleeping face and thinking, "One day he will die and he will be buried, but I will be alive."

His ambivalence about his father, which had made him arrive late for his funeral, is rather like his ambivalence about Rome, which he both longs and fears to visit. After his father's death he had felt strangely uprooted. He was not sure what he wanted or even where he was going. He had been obliged to discover himself anew, to descend into the underworld of his own buried self, to attempt with Fliess to lead him, his Virgil, to discover his own unconscious, in what he came to think of as his self-analysis. It was a difficult time for him. Perhaps his mood swings were also due to his attempts to stop the cocaine he and Fliess had been taking in large doses, and which he now realized was unwise. These objects that he began collecting shortly after his father's death are in some way related to that wild search for self.

All this passion to collect, Fliess has dismissed as a waste of time. "Behind every collector there is a Don Juan," he once said.

Still the girl says nothing, lying there coughing on his couch.

"You do not trust me enough to tell me what comes to your mind?" he asks her.

"Why should I ?" she replies disconcertingly.

"Well, after all, why would you not? I trust you to tell me the truth," he replies.

She sighs and waves her hands and seems to think about his words.

He goes on, "You think I am like your father, or even Herr Z., both of whom you consider, I gather, untrustworthy?" he says.

The girl says, "Well, they have both been your patients, haven't they, and my father is paying you to cure me, isn't he?"

He decides not to answer that, taken aback by her rudeness.

It is possible that he should let the girl settle in for a while longer before bringing up the matter of repressed desire and before explaining how her complaints about her father, their vehemence, are a sure sign of her attachment to him. But he is afraid she might escape without this essential clarification. He is in a hurry to cure her. She is obviously quite perceptive, but just as obviously puffed up with pride, spoiled, and rude. She seems to know a surprising amount about her father's illness.

He stares at this sulky girl, who still has something of the child's glow about her dimpled pink cheeks, her smooth hands, the soft glossy hair, the little ankles he glimpses in her dainty shoes. He cannot help but find her attractive and at the same time infuriating. She is a strange mixture of considerable acumen and childishness. He thinks that children are not the ignorant or innocent beings people like to think they are, though surely they know otherwise. At times he feels he is only discovering what every nursemaid must already know. The truth is, he cannot help finding this pretty, rich girl difficult and disagreeable but also endearing. He is anxious to rein her in.

Instead he asks, "Are there people you can talk to more easily?"

She thinks for a while and says she would find it much easier to speak to a woman.

"A woman? You would trust a woman more than you trust me?" he says, taken aback, offended despite himself. He would like to tell her she ought to be careful with women. She ought to watch out for them, particularly women as intelligent and appealing as she is herself.

He must not be fooled by this young one's considerable wiles. He cannot help thinking sometimes of where his career might have taken him if he had not fallen so desperately in love with Martha. What if he had been able to have a full-time research career? What if he could have continued to work in the quiet of a laboratory with a microscope and something like a lamprey or a crayfish and his own fine mind, instead of having to listen endlessly to these querulous hysterics? He remains proud of his early discoveries, which surely bolstered Darwin's idea that evolution operates conservatively, using the same basic building blocks in more and more complex arrangements. What if he had not followed von Brücke's well-meaning suggestion to enter the clinical practice of medicine? What if he had not had to support such a large family and spend his time listening to patients like this one, he thinks, looking at this spoiled girl shifting around on his couch.

He remembers writing to Martha in the early days of their courtship and referring to women as sorceresses. Her power was such that it seemed almost magical to him in those days. He recalls how he blamed her for preventing him from achieving fame in the cocaine affair, of going to visit her and failing to pursue his findings fast enough, allowing Köller to step in and get the prize for his idea.

"The French fräulein you spoke of, for example? You feel you could trust her?" he asks, aware of the hint of sarcasm in his voice, thinking the girl would have preferred to confer with an ignorant servant girl rather than with a learned medical man, and wondering at the same time what happened there and why the girl had her dismissed.

He is suddenly aware that this girl, with the glow of her youth, her splendid dress, her odor of wildflowers, and her bright mind has somehow brought out his fear of women, their ability to harm and even to destroy. He thinks of his clever old Catholic nurse, the thief, who was always taking him off to church to listen to sermons about hellfire and scolded him for his clumsiness.

"Indeed, I liked her so much. We had so many interesting conversations," she tells him enthusiastically. "We discussed the meaning of life, who we were, and a woman's role in society. *She* encouraged me in my studies and even accompanied me to concerts and to the art galleries," she mentions again loftily. She admires the painter Klimt, whom she saw exhibited with the Secessionists. "I love the frescoes he did at the new Court Theater on the ceiling. Have you seen them?" she asks in her airy way, as though they were at a dinner party. He avoids the question. He says, "I'm not particularly an admirer of modern art, it is ancient art that I find so intriguing." He thinks that it is Rome he would like to visit, not a Klimt exhibition.

He brings her back to the fräulein who has obviously been important in her life.

"Why was she dismissed? What did she do to offend you?" he asks again.

She only says that the fräulein gave her so many interesting books to read.

"Molière, you said. What else?" the doctor asks, recalling what the father told him about the unsuitability of the texts and how they had led the girl astray.

She tells him, sounding rather proud of herself, that she has read Mantegazza's *Physiology of Love.* "All three volumes, which we read in Italian—killing two birds with one stone, my fräulein said, all about the perversions and about men's and women's bodies," she tells him without shame, shifting around on his comfortable couch, smoothing down her skirts over her legs, running her fingers through her soft ringlets, her gold bracelets chinking. "And we discussed them at length." He has obviously struck oil here, he thinks, surprised by this revelation.

With her fräulein, too, she read other advanced books, even foreign ones which she shared with her, she goes on, showing off her erudition, listing them: Flaubert's "Simple Heart," and Dostoyevsky—"I do love Dostoyevsky!" she gushes, "his characters are all so very miserable they make me feel happy in comparison."

"A great writer, Dostoyevsky," he admits.

"And I read *Anna Karenina* by Tolstoy—and even Walt Whitman. My brother gave me von Hofmannsthal—what a good-looking man!" she says. "I caught a glimpse of him in a café in Vienna one evening and almost fell in love with him immediately—and my brother encouraged me to read him.

"My brother does encourage me to learn but when I *do* study, Mother scolds me and says I spend too much time reading. I am not allowed to read in the morning, for example. Can you imagine? I have to sew or do something equally dumb, *dumb*. Otto never really takes my part against Mother or even Father. In the end he is just like Father— and as much as I love him, I have to admit he says one thing but acts differently. He and Father are both such hypocrites! *Hypocrites!* Or anyway they are too timid to stand up for what they believe," she says angrily. Her brother does not dare act in a rebellious way; he does not like a fight, particularly with her mother. He is always the conciliator in the family.

But she could speak most frankly to her French fräulein, about so many things—intimate, womanly things. She says, "In some ways it was easier speaking in another language. Do you know what I mean? And women speak a different language from men, don't you think? It would be much easier, yes, and less frightening to talk to a woman who would understand," she concludes triumphantly and crosses her arms on her chest.

"But not to your own mother, I gather?" the doctor suggests, knowing the answer there.

"No, not Mother," she is forced to concede, but then, annoyingly, takes the pretext to complain at length about her mother.

"I have never really been able to talk to Mother, which is so sad. She doesn't seem very interested in, well—matters of the mind," she says in her pretentious way. "I know she loves me, and she *says* she wants the best for me, and perhaps she really believes she *does*," she says, obviously trying to be fair, "but she doesn't understand my interest in books and the way the mind works, or the answers to so many questions about life that trouble me. I once actually told her we had nothing in common, which was cruel, I know, and she was very hurt, and I'm really sorry for that.

"Poor Mother—it's not really her fault at all, you know. She was given so little education, and she can hardly spell and is often so sick herself with—whatever it is she's got, and she hardly ever opens a book, or only the kinds of books that tell you nothing about life," she says. "It may not be her fault, but she is very ignorant about so many things and she prefers to believe what is convenient, to maintain that everything in life is for the best: '*Tout pour le mieux dans le meilleur des mondes.*'"

"Voltaire?" the doctor hears himself ask.

She rambles on about her mother. "In the end Mother is just as bad as Father, perhaps she's even worse. She never challenges what she *must* know are Father's lies! Why does she not stand up for me, when she *knows* what I say is true! How *can* she be such a coward! Why do women never stand up for one another?" she asks, sitting up in her anger, waving her hands around wildly, her cheeks flushed.

All her mother cares about are the household chores and her own illnesses. When she thinks certain rooms need cleaning, she locks their doors, and makes the servants open the windows, even on the coldest of days. "You would hardly believe my poor brother. He hates to confront Mother. He's such a coward! Once I found him cowering in his room studying, all muffled up in his coat and hat and gloves with the windows wide open in the middle of winter! And when I said, 'What *are* you doing? Are you mad?' He just said, 'It's not so terrible! I'd rather not make a fuss.' At least I shut the windows for him!" she says.

He thinks of his own wife, who has a very similar preoccupation with household cleanliness. He allows her to rule over her domain and does not interfere with the rigid rules for the hours of the meals. He gives her all his earnings to keep in a strongbox and must ask her when he needs money for his cigars or his purchases of antiques, of which she disapproves. He accepts her scolding meekly, if he ever spills or breaks anything or soils the carpets with his muddy shoes. He is a henpecked husband, he considers, though her control is curtailed to domestic matters. He has managed to preserve certain prerogatives naturally, such as having his family travel second class while he rides in first on the trains, in order to travel in peace and quiet and have a moment for his important work.

He has tried to talk to Martha about his work, but she gets

that anxious, distracted look in her eyes as he speaks and doesn't seem to hear what he is saying, or she changes the subject, or often finds some pretext to escape, getting up and leaving the room, going on some absurd household errand or even to the bathroom. He has the uncomfortable feeling she is shocked. Is it possible she considers his theories pornographic? Obviously she does not enjoy discussing his work. And even Minna, who tells him she admires it and often accompanies him to the *Kaffehaus* in the evenings, or on his travels, does not always seem able to grasp the importance of what he is saying. How much easier it is to speak with Fliess, who has a completely open mind and is able to consider any and all possibilities.

But the fräulein and Frau Z. were women she could talk to freely, the girl says.

"And you feel you could trust them?" he asks, aware of what her response will surely be.

"Of course," she admits, "confiding in them did have its disadvantages. What interested the fräulein most, I came to discover, was *love* or what she thought was love. The only reason she was so kind to me, I gradually understood as I got older, and the reason she tried to stir me up against Mother and Frau Z., was because she was attracted to *Father*. When he was present, she was all charm and sweetness, and when he left, she lost interest and dropped me completely like a hot cake. She was only using her intimacy or what I thought was intimacy with me as a way to get closer to Father. Everyone! Everyone is in love with my father! They either want his body or his *money*," she says, lying back down and relapsing into sullen silence, beating her fists against his beautiful rug.

"And you think it is his money I want?" he says eventually.

"Well, in the end, are you not on Father's side?" she asks.

"You don't believe that, as a medical man, a man of science, I have your well-being or, at the very least, a respect for the truth at heart?" he asks, shifting around in his chair. Yet he cannot entirely ignore this young girl's words.

He thinks of what she dared to say about the harm the learned men in the medical profession do. His brilliant mentors come to mind, those men who came before him at the university in Vienna and who blazed a trail, great thinkers like Rokitansky, Meynert, and above all von Brücke, who has influenced him perhaps more than anyone else; what does she know of them? Is she unaware of the reputation of the medical school in Vienna and how people flock there from all over the world?

Still, her comment hit a sore spot. He could not help thinking of poor Emma E. and Fliess's operation on her nose, which came to him in a dream he used in his book. He recalls Emma E. telling him, her voice heavy with sarcasm, "So *this* is the strong sex," when he had almost passed out in her presence. A fainter who frequently succumbs to strong emotion, he had had to leave the room at that moment and restore himself with a glass of strong cognac. He can vividly recall that poor woman's blanched face, her protruding eyes, the clots of blood and the fetid smell, when the surgeon had pulled forth half a meter of gauze that Fliess had left behind in her nose. What overwhelmed him then was the feeling of remorse for having recommended this surgeon to her in the first place. Why had he not realized what was happening?

When Mathilde had once put a bead up her nose, he had divined the problem quickly enough from the odor. He does not intend to make that mistake again.

Was the operation entirely necessary? He thinks how the woman had come to him with her vague symptoms of nosebleeds, depression, and menstrual cramps and how he had sent her to Fliess who had removed the turbinate bone from her nose and transformed her entire face with the operation. He has let Fliess operate on his own nose twice. His operation on Dora Breuer, too, was most successful. The young girl who, come to think of it, is about the same age as his new patient, was very grateful. But poor Emma will never look the same again. Yet the dear woman does not seem to hold it against either of them, and indeed, is particularly interested in psychoanalysis.

"But you *are* on father's side. He has brought me here, and he is paying you to get me to do as he wishes, to go along with his plans. He is just using me as bait!" she says.

"Your father has his intentions, no doubt, and I certainly have mine, but surely we have the same goal: your health and well-being and the cessation of your symptoms and your suffering. My goal is only to find the truth, a truth that you may not yet know or wish to recognize."

"But is it not a truth that is convenient for you and perhaps also for Father? Is it not a truth you *want* to believe?"

She goes on, "What do you really think of Father? Do *you* trust him? Does it not just suit you like my mother to pretend to believe him? You must know all about his ailments. And now, if I have understood rightly, Mother suffers from the same shameful ailment, too, which is why we both have to go to stay in the big boring old hotel in Franzenbad to take the turbid baths and drink the acrid waters and sit at endless meals in the hotel dining rooms with all the other old, rich, sick people. Mother's body is weeping, weeping because of my false father! And my own body weeps, too!" she admits.

He listens to her words, watching her open and close her reticule and dip her fingers repeatedly inside. He is conscious of what she is saying, her fingers chattering, giving him their message wordlessly.

"And you don't think you might be responsible yourself for this?" he asks her.

"What do you mean?" she asks.

"Have you not perhaps been touching yourself for your own pleasure, your own hidden and secret desire, and causing this discharge that comes from such unhealthy practices? Can you admit to this? To be honest with yourself is good practice, I assure you."

"I don't know what you're talking about!" she says angrily, her face very red, her eyes flashing as she sits up on the couch, reminding him again of his first love, Gisela Fluss, in her furor.

"Was this not the reason why you have gone from one doctor to the next, afraid they might find your secret, your shameful secret of private pleasure, rather than their incompetence?" he asks, rather pleased with his powers of observation.

As the girl leaves his room, dragging her foot, she does not even look up at him or acknowledge his presence in any way. She does not bother to shake his hand, let alone bob the little curtsey she has obviously been taught is polite with an adult in his position. He sighs and can only hope he has not said too much too fast, that she will come back.

VII

SECRETS

She pushes open the door slowly and looks inside the room. There is no one there. She goes into their well-polished and silent drawing room with its closed velvet curtains and well-dusted artificial hydrangeas on the mantelpiece. She stands still in her coat and hat and leather gloves, only the afternoon noises from the street coming to her. She goes over to the shiny grand piano and surveys the room. She bows to an imaginary and applauding audience. The audience applauds louder and louder as she takes off her gloves slowly, strips off her coat.

She is giving a concert in a great concert hall. She is wearing a splendid green satin gown. She smiles and bows to the applauding audience and sits down very upright and opens up the shiny grand piano. She takes out her music, adjusts the height of the stool, and strikes the keys loudly with aplomb. She is playing the difficult Mozart sonata in A minor that she admires, touching the keys with emotion, playing with brio, until she stumbles and plays a wrong note. Then she gets up and goes out the door and comes back into the drawing room and bows again to the applauding audience, and starts over again. She repeats this performance again and again, until finally her mother puts her head around the door and says, "Darling, do you think you could possibly play something else?"

She bangs the piano shut, gets up, and drags herself up the stairs, both her legs aching terribly, a burning pain down her side, her breathing labored. She goes to her room, slams the door shut, and throws herself onto her canopied bed and weeps. She has pain down both legs, her stomach cramps, and she is coughing. What good does this doctor do, she thinks as she pounds her pillow. Perhaps electricity, cold baths, brushes thrust down her throat, or even hypnosis would be preferable to him! At least they would not make her feel guilty! Anything is better than that! How *can* she continue to go back into that small, smoky room with all its mysterious, ancient objects, its books on the beginnings of civilization, and that horrible, horrible man!

She gets up and runs her fingers fast over her own books in the bookcase above her desk and finds Goethe's *Sufferings of Young Werther*. She has read it several times with delight. The young hero—though she is not quite sure just how young he is—suffers as she does. He feels life with the same passionate intensity. The book, she is certain, though she is a girl and probably younger than the hero, was written for *her. For her.* Reading those pages, feeling all the things young Werther feels gives her a warm feeling, a feeling of not being so entirely alone. Like her, young Werther has little time for the insincere, boring, snobbish people around him, people who are perhaps interested in his mind but not his young heart. The young Goethe wrote these letters just the way she writes her diary, she is certain, to tell the truth about life, though the letters were made up just as her diary is.

She takes out the little key she keeps hidden among the book's precious pages. She opens the drawer to her desk, where she keeps her diary, a fat, well-thumbed book with a blue leather cover. She sits down before her desk, writing feverishly.

She has kept a diary since she was twelve or perhaps thirteen. She doesn't write every day and she only writes down what she *imagines* and would like to see happen, rather than the real events of her life, which are so monotonous and boring. When her mother found her diary and thought her made-up account was true, she was very shocked! "Why on earth would I write about my own boring real life?" she had asked her mother, who looked hurt. And she has even given herself a new name in the diary: Stella Schonbrunn; Stella, which she knows means star in Italian, and Schonbrunn for the summer palace of the imperial family, with its wonderful park and all the animals. A grand name for a girl who will, she is certain, be grand one day.

She writes the name at the top of each page in ornate script with large loops and curls on the *S*'s. Just doing that makes her feel better, open to new possibilities. She finds that pretending to be someone else, SS, allows her to say things she would never dare say otherwise, and do things on the page she would never dare do, though she often feels and thinks just what SS—as she thinks of herself—does. She likes the double *S*, which entwines like two amorous snakes. She has even drawn them, thick cobras, their heads turned toward one another, tongues entwined, and colored the entwined snakes in gold and green with shiny scales like a Klimt painting. Come to think of it, they are like her and her brother when they were small and would touch their tongues together and then laugh.

Sometimes, she does other little drawings on the pages, though she has never been good at drawing. There is even one of her mother's new green hat that Frau Z. made, which she thought was ridiculous, with its long feather, and sometimes she does drawings of herself doing handstands, which she would do secretly when her legs were not in such pain, or other not at all ladylike things which she likes to do when no one is looking. At the end of some of the entries she has written: "By an undiscovered genius!"

Today she writes: "I feel excitable and vehement, both of which are entirely justified. Sometimes, I think I exist just to get in a rage! I know I'm young but surely I understand much more than the adults around me do!"

She feels this diary is the only place where she is still free to make things up as she wishes, things she can control, in order to recapture something from her wonderful, wild, rebellious days as a child. Here she can see in her imagination what the adults around her cannot punish her for.

Here she has her young engineering student come to her as she runs from Herr. Z. at Lago di Garda. Together they will take the ferry across the lake.

"Suddenly, he is there beside me, looking down at me with his large brown eyes. I stare back at his fresh, flushed cheeks and adorable dimples as he smiles delightfully at me. I like his young and innocent face, his tense, taut muscles, the way he stands on one foot, leaning back against the railing of the ferry."

They take it to a small island, surrounded by willows which trail their branches in the water. As they stand side by side in the wind, holding onto the railing, they watch the waves slap against the side of the ferry, and the spray rise in the air. The ferry, by a strange coincidence, is also called *La Stella*. She can see the white painted letters on the side of the boat. She smells the murky odor of the lake water and sees a rainbow in the spray. The student leans across and takes off her gray glove slowly and carefully, peeling it back like the skin of a fruit and as though he were unsheathing something precious, a fragile soul, to be handled with care. He does not let go of her hand.

She writes:

"On the island, in the shadows of the overhanging willows, we strip off all our clothes. Quickly, I wade into the water, and he follows me. We walk naked into the warm water up to our waists, our chests, toes sinking into the mud. I turn to splash his pale chest. His shoulders are beautifully broad and pale. His fair curls are on his forehead. We dive down together into the depths, kissing below the surface."

That would be something too sacred to tell the doctor.

She knows what he would say about this scene and what she really wants and it is certainly more than the touch of the young man's hand. He doesn't understand that that is really what she wants. She does feel desire, but it is a vague, diffuse feeling spread all over her body. She blots her words and closes her diary, sitting at her desk and looking out the window at the gray winter sky striped with the pink of the sunset. She feels it is a sky of the end of the world.

In reality, she did meet someone that summer at the lake, but not the engineering student whom she had met at a party at her Aunt Malvine's house. Her aunt's husband, who also comes from Budapest, had invited the young student, who loves music as much as she does, and who intrigued her immediately in his extravagant cloak and big butterfly-shaped bow tie. She was standing talking to her uncle in the small garden of their villa in Dobling—it was when her aunt and uncle lived in the nineteenth district—as the violet and gold evening floated around them, when they heard a lightweight carriage rolling up with a clatter of hooves. They watched someone lithe and fair haired, in an elegant gray suit and cloak, spring down fast and walk up the short path from the garden gate toward the front door, his hair worn long and somewhat wild about his head. Her uncle greeted him and introduced them. Then someone called out to her uncle from the lit interior so he left them together in the gloaming of the garden. The student told her he came from Budapest and that his parents had both died there when he was very young. "How sad," she said, moved for him, imagining the little boy alone. He had been brought to Vienna by the great actor von Sonnenthal. "Despite his modest beginnings, he has been made a nobleman by the emperor because of his great art. I admire him immensely," he says. "He has brought me up, though naturally I don't see him very often except on the stage. Have you ever seen him perform?" the young man asked her, and she was obliged to shake her head. "Oh, you must come one evening with me to the Burgtheater and see him do Mortimer in *Maria Stuart*. Would you come with me as my guest one evening perhaps?" he asked, and she smiled back at him and said she was not sure her family would allow that.

He spoke of his desire to become a composer. He plays several instruments including the piano, the fiddle, the trombone, and even the organ and makes extra money for his studies playing at weddings and balls and even at the Zoo restaurant. Perhaps one day he will be able to conduct and have his own orchestra, he said. She listened to the melodious sound of his slightly accented voice as he spoke to her in German, and the garden grew dark. She was touched by his orphaned state, his wild hair, his wild dreams, and wanted to help and protect him.

Later she was to realize she had overlooked his inability to face reality.

Unlike the doctor, in their brief and secret meetings her young student has told her that she is beautiful and brilliant, pure and good, and that he wants to spend his life with her. She has not mentioned this to her father as the man is just a student, an orphan with no money and no real prospects, or even much interest in the engineering he is supposed to be studying. She is afraid her father would not approve. But she has met him in secret at the museum, and once they went to the theater together to see Adolf von Sonnenthal, and he took her backstage afterward to meet the great actor. She was sorry she had gone, as she realized he was not at all a handsome man, but seemed able to transform himself into whatever he wanted on the stage. Her student sends her letters and sometimes postcards from Budapest when he returns there, which she treasures and hides in her desk, locked away in the folds of her secret diary.

Why does she have to remain immobile on the doctor's couch, day after day, just to be told that everything is her fault! What sort of creature will emerge from his silken cocoon at the end of her time there—the doctor has said it might be a year! When she does come forth she will be transformed into something small, pale, and deformed, a slug, something no man would want anyway, worming its way across his silky carpet, leaving behind its trail of misery like a snail's trail.

Why should she believe that her illness is her own fault, brought about by *masturbation*. (The very sound of the word seems shameful to her and makes her shudder.) She wonders how sick she really is. If she manages to relax her whole body she can almost make the pain go away completely. But *how* can one concentrate like that continuously? The pains come and go so mysteriously. At one moment she feels her whole body wracked with pain and then at others she feels nothing. Sometimes if she manages to walk in the woods on a spring day she feels so much better, looking up into the trees, studying the birds, feeling part of the nature around her.

Just lying there, listening to the doctor mention hidden

desires, makes her want to touch herself, it is true. She has done it from time to time in bed, unable to sleep, where she makes up strange stories with pictures to accompany her gestures. Her fantasies, like her diary, are also a place of freedom, though they make her feel guilty, which her diary does not. She has never written down her fantasy or told the doctor about that! There is always a little boy in her stories and a beating.

Over and over again she makes up this same beating fantasy sometimes with some small variations. Sometimes the fräulein wears a blue skirt and not a brown one. Sometimes she has an assistant, a young blond man whom she calls upon to beat the little boy with a stick when he is bad, or sometimes he even gives the boy an enema as punishment, but parts of the story are always the same. The little boy is always sitting in a big bay window in the sunlight when the fräulein comes bursting into the room in her long dark dress that rustles as she walks. The little boy can hear the sound of her long petticoats and see the skirt that froths like foam around her slender ankles as she comes over to him, and he knows what she will make him do as she holds him in her arms.

Without the doctor making her feel even worse with his words, she always feels very guilty afterward, as much for the strange story she has made up as for the actual touching.

She remembers her fräulein lying next to her on the bed once while she crossed her legs with her hand between them, her whole body trembling with pleasure. The fräulein said, "What on earth are you doing?"

"Just scratching," she had lied, not really aware of what

she was doing, though suddenly realizing this was not acceptable behavior.

As she thinks about it now, sitting at her desk in the late afternoon with her diary before her, she runs her hands over her body. She feels the slight swell of her new breasts, her stomach through her wool dress, the strangeness of it all. Is this me? Who is this girl? What does she want?

She pulls up her white skirt and petticoats and slips her fingers down beneath her long underwear and between her legs and holds herself tight, holding on to herself as though she might otherwise disappear. At the same time she conjures up images:

A boy child sits alone in the sunlight in a bay window. He hears the sound of his fräulein's long skirts rustle as she comes into his big empty room in her brown dress. The fräulein looks around the room disapprovingly and says as she always does: "What is going on here?" which already makes the boy feel guilty though the bare room is very clean and tidy, not a toy out of place.

"Have you been a good boy?" the fräulein asks in her accented German.

"Oh, yes, very good," he says, as always.

Then she smiles at him sweetly with her large glistening mouth, her lips very red, and undoes her bodice and then her tight low-cut blouse letting her heavy breasts swing free. "Come, let me see," she says, and she gathers him up in her arms and holds him close against her soft body. She thrusts her thick brown nipple into his mouth and tells him to suck.

"No! No!" he says, trying to turn his face away, with

disgust, but she holds him too tightly and then he does suck as he always does with more and more pleasure. When his body responds to this, she says disapprovingly, touching him in his private place, making him swell and swell, "Well, well, look at you! I don't call that a good boy, do you? No! No! Not a good boy at all," and she turns him over on her knees and beats him on his buttocks and tells him he is a naughty, naughty boy.

Then the man who is usually young and fair haired and beardless like her engineering student changes in the picture into an older, dark-haired man with intense eyes, emerging from the shadows of the room. At first she thinks it might be Herr Z., but then she recognizes him with a little shiver. It is the doctor himself, looking grim and cross, piercing her with his deep disapproving gaze, grunting and straining and sweating a little in his starched white shirt and mournful bow tie as he bends over her to gather her up and hold her hard, asking her if she has been a good girl, then he is turning her over his knees, and beating her hard, while he presses his legs against her sex and runs his hands all over her to make her keep still. She gasps a little, her fingers damp, and lets her head lean back against the hard chair.

She wonders if the doctor touches himself sometimes even now. Surely not. She cannot imagine it! And perhaps all he has to suck on are his terrible, foul-smelling cigars. Perhaps that is his problem. He seems a very controlled and diligent person and probably did not dare touch himself anymore, even as a child, once his nursemaid or his mother had told him it was dangerous, that it would make his penis drop off, or would make his brains rot. Perhaps he is not even able to make love to his wife anymore. Does the doctor have sexual intercourse with his wife, she wonders, and thinks that probably he does not and that is why he wants his patients to talk so much about their secret desires.

VIII

SUBTERFUGE

To his surprise she does come back the very next day, and on time, sweeping into his office, looking flushed and a little disheveled. On such a cold day, her head is uncovered, her long, glossy hair whipped by the wind, in unruly curls on her shoulders, her cheeks pink. She lies on his couch, fidgeting distractedly, pulling at her gloves, and coughing from time to time as she goes on talking monotonously about her father's lies. *That* is what is making her ill, she insists.

"Which ones this time?" he asks, stifling a yawn.

She says she will tell him if he really wants to know. She might just as well get it over with.

"Start away," he says.

She tells him about what she calls the "subterfuge." She explains how she and her family had met the Z.'s in the spa town south of Innsbruck. Actually, it was thanks to her that they all met.

He notices with some satisfaction that she seems for the first time willing to answer him, to talk of the Z.'s, speaking more easily without coughing as much. He is finally getting somewhere, he thinks, despite her bad temper, and relaxes a little in his chair, listening to her tale with interest.

"It was their little girl I noticed first, actually," she says. She was having tea on the terrace of a hotel in Meran one afternoon with her parents. They had gone there for a treat— perhaps it was even her mother's birthday—she doesn't remember exactly, she says, or perhaps it was simply because of the splendid view over the valley. She was sitting on the terrace, feeling bored, when she first noticed the family. She was eating creamy chocolate cake and drinking cool lemonade. Her brother was not there, and she missed him particularly as there were no other children. She looked up and saw the couple enter with their two children: the little boy, fair headed and rosy cheeked like his mother, in whose arms he wriggled, and the pale, dark-haired girl, who held her father's hand and looked so old-fashioned as she gazed at them with her large eyes.

From the start the child intrigued her. There was something so serious and contained about the small girl, and she had felt from that moment that something might happen to her, though she wasn't sure what it might be.

Besides, she has always liked playing with younger children, teaching them, playing school, and this little girl had such a strange and grave expression.

The Z.'s were led to a less favorable table than theirs, she remembers, one with limited shade that hot summer afternoon. She watched the little girl with her old-fashioned face, her dark hair tied back from her high forehead, whom she caught staring at her with her light blue eyes. She looked like a child in an old painting, sitting there so quietly, unnaturally still for someone that age. Hardly moving, she seemed pinioned by the white mountain light, her skin almost transparent. Her stillness contrasted with her wriggling brother, who was making a terrible fuss, kicking his red boots against the table leg and spreading strawberry jam all over his smart sailor suit. A little boy who couldn't keep still, she says.

"The little girl smiled at me and slipped suddenly from her wicker chair in her smocked sundress with its little wing-like sleeves—I can see it all so clearly—and came running over to our table. She stood beside me and stared up at me as I ate my chocolate cake. I looked over at the child's mother, who was trying to cope with the naughty boy. I asked if I could share my cake with her little girl. Frau Z., for it was she, the mother, smiled graciously, nodded her head in assent, and laughed a little at her daughter. Frau Z. is, I will admit, very lovely when she laughs, perhaps you know, her mouth very red and her teeth unusually white and even," she says.

"How old were you?" the doctor asks.

"I was twelve years old—almost thirteen that summer, I think, and the little girl, Clara, must have been around three or four.

"After that we often met in the town where the Z.'s lived. Herr Z. had a shop there, which you probably know, and Frau Z. made hats. She is very gifted with her hands. She makes wonderful, extravagant hats with wide brims, feathers, and ribbons, and once even with a fake bluebird, although she, too, was often ill and had to go away one summer to a sanatorium. Mother bought several hats in their shop, for her and also for me. Together Father and Frau Z.—Pippina, she told me to call her—took the 'grape cure,' the curative grapes, which grow in the area, and sometimes they took the 'whey cure' in the summers, and the waters and the baths for all their ailments. Or we just met on the Wassermauer, the promenade, in the old town," she tells him.

"Both Herr Z. and his wife were exceptionally kind to me," she admits. "At first I wasn't sure which one I liked better. At first, in my ignorance, I thought they were so kind because I was precocious and well read, so clever and amusing. They made me feel I was an especially gifted child. What an idiot I was!" she says bitterly. They both made her feel so pretty and bright. They invited her to quote the poetry she knew by heart and marveled at her memory. Or they asked her to play the piano, which she did gladly for them.

Much of the time, though, she had sat beside her father in the dark room when he had trouble with his eyes and recited poetry for *him*.

"Then Frau Z. began nursing Father, too—'You go outside and play with the children. They would love that. They are so fond of you, and you are too young to have to sit for such long hours in a dark sickroom,' she would say to me when Father was very sick and when Mother felt incapable of helping, and Father refused to have a nurse," she says. "I thought her so kind and thoughtful! And I was so happy to play outside with her children. I've always loved both of them but particularly the little girl, who would follow me around like a shadow. I taught her how to say some things in French and play simple pieces on the piano."

One summer they had all left Meran and gone on holiday together to a hotel on beautiful Lago di Garda in Italy. "Frau Z., Pippina, comes from northern Italy, perhaps you know, from the lake country," she says. "And I think it was she who chose the luxurious hotel at the lake where we all spent that summer. I had not quite turned thirteen."

She will never forget the place, she says: the laughter at the tables on the terrace; the sparkling white wine she was allowed to sip for the first time; the dark-haired, hard-working Italian waiters who huddled in a corner by the bar in the shadows, waiting for the first guests to arrive when the restaurant doors swung open in the evening. "They would watch me as I entered, staring as I walked across the terrace to our table, and making me blush to the roots of my hair."

She remembers the large balcony off their room with its round wicker table and chairs, where Pippina had patiently taught her to play endless games of honeymoon bridge, the game that would one day save her life. From the start she took to bridge where she starred and was able to exercise her excellent memory, and she had a feel for cards, which Frau Z. would praise profusely. "You remember every card played, don't you?" she would say, watching her with admiration. "And I do," she tells the doctor proudly. " 'This child is amazing! What a memory! She's quite brilliant!' Frau Z. would exclaim, which made me so happy."

"Yes, and what happened there that summer? You spoke of subterfuge," the doctor says, hoping she will not be sidetracked again by accounts of her intellectual prowess. What a show off! But she takes her sweet time, showing off her descriptive powers, her vocabulary in various languages.

"I don't know why," she says, "but I remember that place so clearly, perhaps it was because I got my period there for the first time—not that anyone said much about that! Except to explain at length the hygiene involved and to make me feel I was much too young for this to have occurred.

" 'I was sixteen,' Mother kept saying disapprovingly, as though this visible sign of being a woman were somehow a fault or at any rate a weakness."

She remembers the hotel's shadowy pine forest on one side and its lawns that run down to the scintillant water, the elegant guests with their parasols sauntering indolently across the smooth green grass in the glare of white light.

They all took the train together from Meran, she says. He thinks of his early train journeys and remembers the glimmerings of the lamps, the overnight train trip, and the glimpse of his mother's white body in the dark of the compartment as they voyaged to Vienna for the first time, this city which he both hates and loves.

But the girl is lovingly describing her arrival at the lake hotel. They were ushered through the high-ceilinged halls and up the stairs to the bedrooms and along a white corridor, with the bellhops carrying all their many suitcases—they were there for a month, she says. Little Clara and Otto—"Their little boy has the same name as my brother, which made him all the more dear to me," she says—who had been cooped up during the long train ride, skipped joyously ahead, hand in hand, the silent corridor now ringing with their laughter and cries. She remembers the slight smell of disinfectant soap and, when the bellhop opened the doors on the rooms, the puffy white counterpanes on all the beds, the flowers fanned in silver vases, the large windows with the silky green curtains caught back with golden ropes, the balconies on each of the big sunny rooms, and the view of the sparkling lake below.

"It was a little like a dream—or perhaps even paradise at first. It seemed the loveliest place in the world," she says. She recalls how the children went running from one room to the next, taking off their shoes and bouncing on the beds and then joining hands and singing the Italian song they had learned from their mother, something like 'Giro giro tondo, Casca il mondo, they all fall down!' And then lying flat on their backs on the beds and laughing."

"So, you were happy there?" he asks, imagining the lovely place and wishing that it were summertime and that he were free and could leave this small room and his chair to go walking in the mountains, which he loves, looking for mushrooms with his own children. What if he had the means to take his own family to that lake that he knows well and admires?

He thinks, too, of the freedom of his own early childhood in Freiberg, the clucking of the poultry, the blue-gray hills in the distance, the sweet fragrance of the fields, the river, the throbbing song of the larks, his mother's youthful form bending over him adoringly. He has never escaped his longing for this lost paradise, the beautiful woods of his early home. He thinks of how all of that came to an abrupt end when he was hardly four years old. But the girl is going on about the light on the Lago di Garda.

"I was *so, so* happy to be there in that lovely place with the Z.'s, who had been so kind to me! I was happy to be with their children, particularly the delicate little girl, who loved me so much and whom I loved, still love so much." Her father had reserved suites for both the families and also several smaller rooms at the end of the corridor for her fräulein and her own beloved Otto whom she was hoping would arrive in a few days.

At first, each family occupied its own sunny suite: a large bedroom and sitting room for the parents adjoining a smaller one for the children. The nights were deliciously cool; the beds soft and comfortable, with puffy white eiderdowns; the breakfasts of café-au-lait, fresh rolls and brioches, and baskets of fruit were brought to their rooms; the long walks along the edge of the lake with the little children running ahead were joyful. She told them stories, and they played imaginary games: she was Marie Antoinette escaping the revolutionary soldiers, or she was Persephone collecting flowers when Hades comes to kidnap her and carry her off to the underworld, to Hades. How they laughed!

In the evenings after dinner, she was allowed to walk with the grown-ups into the small town for the *passegiatta*, as Italians do, carried along by the flow of people down the main street, everyone chatting and flirting. She would often walk a little behind with Herr Z., who would talk to her about books—she was reading von Hofmannsthal, who had begun publishing his poetry at such a young age, and she felt very grown up and important. He knew some lines by heart and would quote to her, she remembers:

"You are the garden locked / Your childlike hands are waiting / Your lips are without violence"—while her mother would walk ahead with Frau Z. in one of her elegant hats, and her father and sometimes other friends. Frau Z., of course, spoke Italian as well as German and sometimes Italians joined them after dinner, simple people who laughed loudly and had a good time.

"I suspected that it was Father who was paying for both families because the Z.'s, I knew, were not as wealthy. I was so pleased by what I thought of as Father's generosity to these people whom I liked, and who said they liked me so much. Everyone seemed in such high spirits. What a fool I was!" she exclaims.

"Then, one evening, suddenly everything changed. Father announced something that upset me terribly. The evening had started out so well. Mother had, unusually, allowed me to stay up for dinner and eat with the grown-ups. We were all sitting outside on the terrace at a round table in the splendid restaurant that looked over the lake, the sky lit up by all the stars shimmering in the blue night sky.

"Frau Z. was looking more beautiful than ever, with the perfect oval of her face and her mysterious smile. She is a beautiful woman, I know, and she seemed to me particularly lovely that night. It was warm, and her white, smooth shoulders and arms were bare, and she had a new sickle-shaped pin which glittered in her fair hair. Probably Father had bought it. I remember it all so clearly," she says.

The fräulein had helped her dress, pulling in her waist tight, and even putting her hair up, and her mother had allowed her to wear her best white dress, with the décolleté—"I was starting to have something to show off at that point," she says, putting her hands to her chest and her string of pearls. Her father had even placed her at the table in the best position—or what he probably considered as such, between himself and Herr Z. and with a good view of the lake.

"I felt so grown up. Father said to Herr Z., looking at me, 'Well, look who is the little lady tonight.' And Herr Z. said, 'Indeed,' and smiled at me and said that I looked, well, so pretty. I blushed, but I felt for a moment the center of attention, all eyes on me, like being at your own birthday party, if you know what I mean?"

He says nothing to that and so she continues.

"As the grown-ups were sipping their sparkling white wine, and we were all eating dessert—I still remember what it was—a delicious, sweet blancmange—Father stroked his mustache with his two fingers, the way he does, you know"— and she copies the gesture for him—"and said calmly that he needed a quieter place to work and that, since he often rose in the night and might disturb the family, he had decided to move down the corridor into one of the smaller rooms.

" 'I'll take the room reserved for Otto, as his highness has apparently decided not to grace us as yet with his company,' he announced.

"At first I wasn't quite sure what this meant, or I didn't want to know. I looked across the table at Mother to see her reaction, but she lowered her gaze and said nothing, as usual.

They just went on eating their blancmange," she recounts bitterly. "Then I watched Pippina in her low-cut black dress, her thick blond hair arranged in soft ringlets around her face, smiling slightly ironically at Father. It all seemed unbelievable to me in a way, and for a moment I thought I might not have heard Father's words correctly, with them sitting there so calmly and going on eating their food as if nothing had happened, while I was trembling, terrified by what this might mean, that my suspicions might be confirmed."

"Of course," he says.

"The very next day, after Father had moved down the corridor, Frau Z. did, too, as I was so afraid she might. The fräulein was brought to sleep in the room with the children on the pretext that they were keeping the couple up, and Frau Z. moved into the fräulein's small single room at the end of the corridor, on some excuse of exhaustion, so that she and Father were each sleeping alone and opposite one another and thus could quite easily go into one another's rooms."

"And this is why you are so angry with your father? Because you are jealous of Frau Z.?" he asks her.

"If that was all he had done, I wouldn't be here today, I don't imagine," she says crossly.

IX

MINNA

THE DOCTOR IS LOOKING THROUGH his letters on the silver salver in the entrance hall, his hands shaking. Still nothing from Fliess, he sees, and his heart tilts with sadness.

He stands for a moment in the hall, gathering himself together. Whom will he confide in, if not his beloved friend? Women have never filled this role for him. Perhaps there were too many around him as a boy, too many sisters, one arriving after another in quick succession. Now not even his sister-in-law, the passionate Minna, fulfills that role, he thinks as he enters the dining room and is glad to find her well enough to sit in her habitual place at the breakfast table. He has worried about her after the necessary intervention and her stay in the spa in Meran.

He takes his place in silence at the head of the table, nodding to his wife and his sister-in-law and wishing the children a good morning. The two women sit in silence, facing each other on either side of him with the six children all sitting meekly upright around the table, waiting for their father to begin eating. His soft-boiled egg is waiting for him, getting cold, he sees, in its porcelain eggcup. He is the only one who has the privilege of a daily egg, on the pretext that he needs to keep up his strength. Sometimes he will cut off the top and give it to the child sitting nearest to him.

The honey shimmers golden, the butter shines, wrapped in its green leaf. He can smell the fresh, warm kaiser rolls. Everything in its appointed place. Martha gives him a disapproving glance, purses her lips, and glances at the clock, because he is a few minutes late, and they have all been waiting. Then she pours the coffee and the frothy hot milk from the large blue porcelain pitchers with the gilt edges she brought from her own home and passes them down the table.

He glances at Minna, widening his eyes with mock guilt, pulling his lips down at the sides. His sister-in-law has long been his ally and companion on his extended voyages. Almost from the start he has used her, first to pry Martha free from her possessive family and an undesired closeness with her mother, and now for other purposes.

Minna looks at him with a little laugh in her dark, sloe eyes and a slight smile of complicity. Such an intelligent woman, the younger, taller sister is, with her narrow, jolie-laide face, her thick braid of silky hair, her arched nostrils, her sly, slanting, mocking eyes. She watches him from across the breakfast table, as Martha breaks off the end of a roll in disapproving silence.

How much does his Martha know about his closeness with her sister? How much does she condone? How much is simply convenient for her to ignore? Perhaps she, too, prefers to keep all this safely and quietly, and above all disease-free, within the family and under the same roof, occasionally sending him off with her blessing on his voyages of exploration with her energetic younger sister to let off some steam. How much of this is partly a relief to her, freeing her, as it does, from his unwanted nightly urges? A prudent and sensible woman, his little princess has become over the years a woman of tact, intelligence, and control.

Many years later she will be the one who, with her quiet calm, will get the Gestapo to give up their guns and sit down in their living room by telling them firmly that they never keep guests standing in their home. She will tell them to help themselves to the large amount of cash they have on hand, which will call forth his remark about never having been paid so much for one session.

Now he thinks of her unexpected arrival that day at the hut on Mount Rax. At first he had thought it was an apparition—she had always said she was not able to hike to that altitude, but then he had realized it was his wife who had followed him, standing in the low doorway, looking flushed and pretty in her dusty boots, delighted with her prowess and with the splendid view. How happy she was, how grateful for his promise to leave her free, to have her life back, after six children in eight years, after his promise of abstinence.

It is the only way. He remains opposed to coitus interruptus and to masturbation and even to the use of condoms, which he finds too difficult to use and are not reliable anyway. Besides, his frequent failures and distressing performances with his wife recently make him prefer abstinence with her.

The sexual side of his marriage, he thinks sadly, has been amortized.

He doubts that Fliess's wife is able to help him much in this way, either. He knows Breuer has planted the seed of jealousy in that woman's narrow mind and seeks to stir up trouble between the two. How strange that Fliess's wife and his young patient should have the same name, not a name he likes particularly.

He has to admit though that things are proceeding nicely and quite easily with this new patient at last. Despite a difficult beginning she is proving easier, or perhaps he is more experienced than he was with Ilona W., though she was one of his most successful cures. He still remembers the satisfying glimpse he caught of her dancing, once he had uncovered her repressed love for her brother-in-law, a girl who had come to him unable to walk.

This one, too, seems to be walking and above all talking more easily. The locks are opening to his key now, he has written to his friend.

He sees it all quite clearly and he already feels this case will be one to help him prove his theories and achieve the fame he so desperately seeks.

He knows his prudent Martha, who eats her roll and butter and sips her hot coffee so daintily in silence at his side, would like him to receive the professorship, which would bring both prestige and higher fees at last. She, too, is impatient for his success. He thinks of Goethe's words, "Decorations and titles ward off many a shove in the crowd." Martha, despite her tact and her sweetness, is no fool. It was she who suggested he send his book on dreams to an influential colleague. "Perhaps I should write first and ask if he'd like to read it?" he had asked.

"No, no, just send it. Who can resist picking up a book and at least reading the first page or two?" she had replied. Women, he realizes, can be a definite help as well as a hindrance in his career.

They have ridiculed his book on dreams. No one will accept the simple truth that all dreams conceal wishes. Why is it that human nature denies what they can see so clearly before their eyes? Well, he will give them some indisputable proof. All he needs now from this girl are a few dreams. How he would like to discuss this case with Fliess!

Fliess's wife is jealous of her husband's close relationship with him, just as this patient seems to be jealous of her father's friendship with the Z.'s. Yet he still dreams of going to Rome with Fliess. He thinks of Rome, like the mind, as a place with ancient secrets to discover. What could be more pleasurable than discovering the secret streets of that city that he has dreamed of again and again with his magician, the only one besides Minna who has really had faith in his work. Ah, Rome: how he longs to go there! He knows it is a necessary part of his voyage of self-discovery, and yet he fears to go to the city which his childhood hero, the Semitic Hannibal, had never managed to take during his fight against the Romans, which he thinks of as the fight of Jewry against the Catholic church; he thinks of Rome as the city that could be conquered by him who should first kiss the mother as the oracle had foretold.

He eats his buttered roll and sips his coffee in silence as the servant comes and goes in the room. It is Minna who tells young Martin not to chew with his mouth open. The boy looks at his father for support, but the doctor says nothing. How could he contradict her? He remembers the brief, stolen August days they spent in the Schweizerhaus, in Majola, the high, attic room, number 11—he will never forget the number, or the slanting ceiling, or the sunshine coming in and shining on the crumpled sheets, on the bread crumbs from breakfast, and on her long, black hair, tumbling down her smooth, bare back, the beads of perspiration on her long upper lip.

X

PROTEST

"What was going on was perfectly obvious to anyone who had eyes to see, as the fräulein herself said," the girl says, going on with her story without any prompting from him this afternoon.

"Did you say anything to anyone?" the doctor asks.

"Indeed, I did!" she says. "My brother wasn't there, so I couldn't confer with him, and I'm not sure he would have done anything anyway, but I decided to speak to Mother myself. The fräulein encouraged me to speak up, too, for her own reasons, reasons that became obvious to me.

"Walking with Mother by the lake the next day, I pointed this all out to her. 'It's not right! Can't you see that? It's embarrassing and humiliating! How can you just remain silent! The whole hotel knows what they are doing together in the night. You have to say something to Father!' I told her. I was so angry."

But her mother had explained that life was not always as simple as her daughter seemed to think. Men, she said, had to be allowed a certain latitude, at times, and women were obliged to look the other way. Marriage, if it was to go on smoothly, sometimes required certain compromises. She had reason to be grateful to Frau Z., very grateful. Indeed, they all did. She herself should be grateful to Frau Z.

"Why should I be grateful to *her!*" she had asked.

"For saving your father's life," her mother had said dramatically.

When she asked for further details, her mother explained that on an impulse one evening after dinner, Frau Z. had followed her father into the pine forest. She was worried because of certain remarks he had made during dinner that he might take his life. Not far from where she and her mother were walking and talking now, her mother told her, in the dark woods on one side of the hotel, Frau Z. had found her father distraught, walking in the shadows of the tall trees with a gun in his hands, which she had managed to convince him to relinquish. It was thanks to Frau Z. that her father was still alive today and with them, continuing to make their lives so comfortable after all, her mother added, gesturing to the lake and the gardens. What would they all have done without him?

"Obviously, it was all a lot of rubbish, something Frau Z. must have made up. Why did Mother just put up with it? Who would believe such a fairy tale, told to cover up a rendezvous? I certainly didn't. Undoubtedly, they were wandering around in the woods together, holding hands or having sexual intercourse, or doing heaven knows what, and I don't see how my mother could be so blind and foolish! Sometimes I think she doesn't care about Father at all, that it is just an economic arrangement. It's more convenient for her to hand over Father, who is sick anyway, to another woman. Besides, I saw how Father visited Frau Z. whenever her husband was away. He always said he had to leave on business for several days. Everyone knew what was going on, including the fräulein.

"Also, Father gave Frau Z. money and presents, a beautiful amber necklace, and tried to cover it all up by giving Mother jewelry, too, a pair of pearl earrings she didn't even like, and there was a quarrel over that."

Obviously the girl has sharp eyes and ears. He cannot disagree with her on this point or indeed any of the others she brings up about Frau Z. and her father. Her story sounds all too familiar to him.

She seems to take his silence for assent, and it is obviously some relief to her.

She says, without coughing and in a clear voice, "Well, at least *you* don't believe I'm making this all up. At least *someone* will know the truth."

"But you tell me this is not what upset you so much, that there is more to the story?"

"Perhaps I'll tell you sometime," she says and flounces out of the room looking rather pleased with herself and without coughing or dragging her leg. He smiles a little, thinking the locks, indeed, are beginning to open to his key. This may be his most successful cure.

XI

_____ _____

BETRAYAL

SHE LIES BEFORE HIM RESTLESSLY on his couch today, grumbling that he does not seem sufficiently moved by her story.

"You don't seem to take my story about Father seriously enough. I don't know if you fully understand his treachery, and why he brought me here in the first place," she says.

"Perhaps you should explain it more clearly then," he says.

"Surely you understand that Father has just made a bargain with Herr Z. so that he can do whatever he wants to with Pippina?"

"A bargain?" he asks.

"He has given me up to Herr Z. so that he can have Pippina. And worse than that, instead of protecting me, taking my side, which he should as my father, surely, he denies his own obvious behavior! He claims I'm making things up, because it is not convenient for him to believe me. He puts her first. I'm just a pawn in their dirty game. He's just using me, to keep Herr Z. quiet and complicit, and you were brought in to smooth things over," she says bitterly.

The doctor asks her to explain what she means.

"He has handed me over to Herr Z. so that he can do what he wants with his wife, don't you see? And you are to keep me complicit," she says angrily.

"What makes you think this?" he asks and imagines how the father would be horrified to hear her say something of the sort. When she says nothing, he asks her, "Do you really think that your father would have entered into a pact with Herr Z. to hand over his beloved daughter for the favors of Frau Z.?"

She admits it was probably not anything that was ever expressed in so many words. "I don't know what happens in your family, but with us and with many of the people I know, it is not necessary to discuss it. Everything is simply understood by everyone, though nothing is ever said. There is a silent language spoken all the time which has nothing to do with what is actually said. Mother says nothing to Father, though she must see what is going on. That's what is so terrible. No one will protect me, not even you! My poor brother just tells me that we should be happy that father has found some happiness in his life, that we should put up with it, that it is none of our business. It's all very well for him. He's free to go out of the house and spend all day at the university and with my uncle, running around trying to help the workers, but what about me! Am I not a human being with feelings and thoughts? I have nowhere to go and nothing else to think about, and it is driving me mad. Mad! It is all the humbug that makes me so angry with Father, the way he lies while telling me I am fabricating!"

"Ah! But that is just the point," he says calmly, shifting his weight and leaning forward in his chair. "Does it not occur to you that this string of reproaches against your father might actually be directed against yourself? Besides, unfortunately, we cannot always change the outside world as we would like to. You must know that by now. Perhaps your father has not behaved as you would have wished him to do, as an ideal father might have, but there is little we can do about others, after all. But we can do something about our inner selves. We can at least make an effort to understand them, and be honest with ourselves, and that you *must* do if you are to return to health."

"What have I to reproach myself for? I have done nothing wrong except to love them too much!" she says, sitting up and turning toward him, tears coming to her eyes.

He sits back in his chair and turns his head away from her, talking to a spot on the wall. "But can you be so sure?" he asks. He tells her what he is certain of, that such vehement hate is often close to love. It seems to him he has always both hated and loved someone since his very early days, often the same person, as with his nephew, and his friend who has so disappointed him and is fast becoming an enemy, Fliess.

He tells her, "In my experience, it is often when my patients protest most strongly that I know what I suggest is true," and he thinks of how he protested so strongly against the idea of bisexuality. "The great writers knew this a long time ago, did they not? Do you know the line from Shakespeare, 'The lady doth protest too much?'"

She lies back down and seems to think about that. She says

she has read Shakespeare with her fräulein and even knows that famous line from *Hamlet*, but it makes her dizzy to think about it. It makes his whole cluttered room with all its strange statues, its pictures, its many books spin around her alarmingly. "Your words make me feel as if I am disappearing, like Alice down the rabbit hole, as though I hardly exist. If no is yes and hate is love, then who am I? If I cannot trust my own feelings, my own thoughts, how can I know who I am? What is real?" she asks him.

XII

HERR Z.

"What I would like to know is why you are so angry with both these men: your father and particularly Herr Z.?" the doctor says. "What has he done to you to cause your ire?"

Would the doctor believe her if she told him all that had passed between them, she wonders. No one else will believe her. If she tells him what happened, will he just blame her, which is what the adults have done up until now? Will she be able to say the words aloud without being sick?

And why, though he has told her she can choose her subject, does the doctor come back to Herr Z.? He seems particularly interested in him. She wonders if he is still charmed by him as she was herself initially. Herr Z.—Hans, as he has told her to call him—is handsome, she will admit, like her father, but darker haired and darker eyed and of a more solid build. Come to think of it, he looks more like the doctor himself.

Is he still, perhaps, one of his patients, she wonders, lying on his couch. Does he, too, come and lie here where she does? Instinctively she sniffs a little to see if she can smell him, but all she can smell is smoke. Or is he now a friend? Why is it that the doctor always takes his side? He never accuses *him* of hate that is really love or love that is really hate. He never accuses him of anything!

She thinks of how this has been going on for years, of all the confessions the doctor must have heard, so many secrets whispered in this comfortable, bourgeois room, all the many suffering people who have come here seeking relief from pain as she has done, people who were encouraged—well more than encouraged—to unburden themselves, to voice their most intimate thoughts, trusting him and finding themselves speaking of things they didn't even know they knew. Will he keep such secrets safe? What will happen to her if she tells him? She doesn't feel she has much choice. She needs to cure her pain, and if the spilling of her secrets is the only way to do that, she will do it. It is true that she now feels better, that she looks forward to coming here every day and being able to speak truthfully to someone who listens and believes what she has to say. Also, there is something about this man, about his darkly bright eyes that she admires, despite herself.

So she says, "Herr Z. was after me from the start. It happened the first time in his office. I wasn't even fourteen. I haven't ever told anyone about what happened then, and I don't know if I should speak of it now to you, or even if you will believe me. Never having spoken of it, it hardly seems real—almost someone else's secret," she says.

"But you are certain this happened?" the doctor asks, and she hears him lean forward with interest.

"Yes! Yes! How could I make up something of this kind? What on earth for?" She may have forgotten certain moments in her life, but this she will never forget.

Herr Z. had invited her to come with him and his wife to watch the feast of Corpus Christi at Saint Nicolaus, the church on the main square in Meran. It was shortly after the Z.'s had moved to a new house near Herr Z.'s shop that had a little balcony overlooking the square below, where the ceremony would take place. It was almost summer, a warm, sunny day for early June, when the procession took place. They often left Meran for the Italian lakes at the height of the summer, but in June they were still there.

"I remember the organdy dress I was wearing, a new one in a deep blue, sprinkled with little raised dots of white. I had put a posy of fresh flowers at the neck," she says.

"So you dressed up for the occasion?" the doctor says.

"I was only thirteen, and I didn't suspect anything at all!" she replies. Why would she? After all, she often went out with them.

She was just happy to be out of the house, away from her father's sickbed for once, and on such a fine day. She remembers how sparkling and fresh it all was: the white sky, the silvery light, the new green leaves of the linden trees, the daffodils and irises, the smells of early summer in the mountain air, the sound of birdsong, and the rushing of the river. How happy she felt then just to be alive, her body without pain! What she would now give to feel like that! She had dressed up for the spring day and yes, for the children and for both of the Z.'s. "They both always said I was so pretty," she tells him.

She pauses, wondering if the doctor might add something about her looks. She has seen him looking at her with his piercing dark eyes when she enters his office. She wonders what he thinks of her, what goes through his mind as he sits in his chair day after day listening to women talk about their intimate lives, talk about love. Women's lives seem so hard to her, above all so boring. They have so much time on their hands, enough for thoughts which often lead to illness.

She knows from her mother's comments to her father that the doctor once gave his patients massages. "Will he be doing massages?" her mother had asked. What did he feel, she wonders, touching all those warm bodies? She presumes they kept themselves covered up, but still. What does the doctor feel now, listening to her talking about Herr Z.'s desire for her? How can he really be objective about what she might say? How could anyone? Does he desire her?

Today she is wearing a new dark blue skirt and a white blouse with a little décolleté. She crosses her aching legs on the sofa and sighs. She would so like to be free of pain as she was that day in Meran, and she wants, too, to impress the doctor in some way, she thinks, looking at all his learned books. She would like him to like her, to admire her intellectual accomplishments, to be pleased by what she tells him and not so silent and withdrawn.

She tells him she was such an avid reader from an early age, reading whatever she could lay her hands on, whatever told her what life was really like, even if it was considered scandalous. Just like him, she was looking for the truth about life, she says.

"I see," he says and laughs a little at that.

The couple both laughed at things she said, too, and complimented her on being so wise and helpful for her age. Herr Z. was particularly pleased with her when she took care of the two children while their mother, who often said she felt ill, went off with her father, she says.

"So you took care of the children to please your father so that he could be with Frau Z.?" the doctor asks.

She says, "Yes, I did, and also to please Frau Z., but I do also really enjoy being with little children. I like playing imaginary games and making up stories for them. I like teaching them. Often as a child I would play school with my pencils, lining them up in a row and pretending they were my students," she says with a laugh.

She likes the imaginary world where children live most of the time. As a child herself, it was that imaginary world that enabled her to sit patiently for so many hours by her father's bedside. She would make up stories in her mind, pictures she could see quite clearly in the dark. "I would spin out into space like a top, leaving my body behind," she says. She tried to amuse Otto and Clara with her stories. She says she supposed they didn't have enough money to hire a real nursemaid for their children, so they used her. Everyone has used her in a way.

" 'She's just wonderful with the children, a little mother to them,' Herr Z. would say to Father, and I would flush with pleasure. What a fool I have been! Basically I saved them a lot of money and also made it possible for Father to be with Frau Z. by taking care of the children, whom I loved so much," she says bitterly.

But both her father and mother impressed on her how kind it was for a man of his age and accomplishments to take such an interest in a very young girl. Herr Z. brought her presents, too, which she accepted as some sort of recompense for her labors.

"What did he give you?" the doctor wants to know. At times he surprises her by his practical way of looking at things. He mentions the price of things frankly. She has been taught that it is not polite to talk about money or sex.

"Chocolates, jewelry—he even sent flowers every day for a year," she says, exaggerating a bit for effect. He wrote to her as well, when he was away, and often she was the one, rather than his wife, who knew when he was coming home. No one seemed to find this odd.

"Because my parents accepted the situation, I did, too, you know, the way a child does—until it was too late," she says.

The doctor brings her back to the feast day in Meran. "So what happened that day?" he wants to know.

She shifts around on the couch, picks up her reticule and puts it down. She starts to cough and is afraid she will not be able to stop, that she might vomit. She feels sick. "It was so awful, *schrecklich*," a word she often uses. "I thought that Frau Z. and the children would be there, too, of course, to watch the procession. There was no reason for them not to be." However, when she walked into the shop, she realized immediately in the dead quiet of the place that there was no one there. All the employees had left, too, though it was not late, and there was no sign of Frau Z. or the little children. She was immediately suspicious, standing there in the silent, empty place. She stood there nervously at the foot of the stairs, as Herr Z. called out to her that he was just shutting up.

"Where is everyone?" she called back up to him, trying to sound cheerful. He explained that he had given his employees a half holiday because of the religious festival. "Most of them are Catholics," he said, which was probably true.

"It's odd, isn't it? When I was very little I had the wrong impression that Catholics were not considered as good as Jews, as they were so often our servants. But it didn't take long at school to realize I was *so, so* wrong."

"But what happened in the shop?" he says.

"I could hear him closing the shutters and see the shadows falling across the floor of the landing. He told me to wait a moment. He was coming down. Frau Z. and the children would join us a little later. I wondered if I should just go, but didn't want to appear rude. So often when I should have acted, I have felt obliged to do nothing from fear of being impolite.

"There was a smell of dust in the air, a banging of the shutters, then a moment of dead silence. Perhaps he was standing looking down on me from the top of the wooden stairs. I don't know, but suddenly, he came out of the shadows, clattering down the stairs. He clutched me hard to his chest, pressed his lips against mine, and thrust his tongue down my throat. It all happened so quickly. I could only stand there, shaking. He was murmuring words, running his hands all over me, touching my breasts and between my legs, saying that he could not stop himself, that I had bewitched him, laid a spell on him, that surely this was what I wanted, too. It was stronger than he. He was in the grip of *eros*—or some such stupid words. In any case it was all *my* fault. He could not let me go. I was irresistible. And all the time he was pressing his body against me."

She can still feel his arms holding her tightly, pressing her against his hard chest. It was horrifying. She was repulsed by him, the smell of smoke on his breath, his horrid beard scratching her cheek. She was so indignant: how could he behave like that with her, a child! The child of his friend! She was thirteen! She was almost sick. She was so frightened and angry that a man his age could behave in that way that all she could do was to run out the door into the street.

"But you did not speak to your parents?" the doctor asks.

"No, I said nothing to anyone," she says. "I felt so ashamed, so ashamed, I didn't want anyone to know what had happened." Even now she still feels ashamed, and she was certain it would all be blamed on her, whatever she said. She thought that there *must* be something wrong with her, as he had said, that she must be a bad girl for him to do such a thing, to let him do such a thing to her.

"After that, everything changed," she tells him. "I saw the whole world in a different, sick way. I felt that surely no one would want to marry me, that I was soiled. And I didn't want to marry anyone, either, if men were like that. I avoided being on my own with him. Neither of us mentioned what had happened, but every time I passed a couple in the street who seemed to be amorous, I would feel shame and repulsion."

She heaves now with distress, afraid she might vomit, but

the doctor does not seem particularly moved by her words. What a hard man.

He says, "I don't see why you would feel disgust. I know Herr Z., as I said, quite well. He is an attractive man in his prime. You might, of course, have been offended from a moral point of view—a married man and somewhat older than you, but surely your physical reaction was an extreme one?"

"I know I feel everything in extremes, but surely any young girl would have felt what I felt—horribly humiliated? Perhaps I feel more than anyone else but that is how I felt. I saw myself from afar just standing there unable to move, passive, and letting this man, Father's age, as old as—well, as old as you, put his arms around me and press his body against mine, his hands on my lady parts, murmuring those horrible lies in my ear," she says, between coughs and great heaves of breath.

She was so filled with repulsion for him and even more for herself. It was her inability to react to this disgusting man that really upset her. "Why did I not defend myself? Why did I not kick him in his private parts! How could I have let this happen?" she exclaims.

"Is it possible that the reason you let him do what he did was that what you felt was not disgust—or not only disgust, but on the contrary, really desire, something that you could not admit to feeling? A repressed desire? Is that not really what you felt, what you still feel, perhaps, this sensation of a man's body pressing against your own?"

She cannot speak now, coughing and coughing, a grinding pain all the way down both her legs as the doctor goes on asking her if she knows what happens to a man's body when he desires a woman.

She nods her head. "I know, I know," she has to admit, afraid he might explain it to her. Of course she knows, horribly, it is often part of her own fantasies: the little boy who swells as he sucks and is beaten for it. She learned about it long ago, first from her brother who once showed her his horrid white wormy thing and how big it could get if she consented to stroke it. Then she had promised on her sacred honor not to tell anyone, and she never will. And then all of this was confirmed by the books the fräulein gave her, and their intimate conversations, sitting close together in her bedroom on the fräulein's bed and giggling, in the late afternoons, making fun of men with their strange and frightening anatomy. She knows about the whole awful thing, though she is horribly embarrassed at this older man's talking about it to her now. How does he *dare* talk about such disgusting things? Does he find this exciting perhaps? Is his own body swelling at this moment as he maintains Herr Z.'s did, as the little boy's does in her fantasies?

The image of a man's erect part thrusting against trousers comes to her as the doctor suggests that what she felt was not against her chest, at all, that what she still remembers so long afterward was rather lower down on her body, that what she remembers was the thrust of his masculinity.

"No! No! No!" she cries out in rage and distress.

She finds it difficult to leave his room, dragging her leg painfully, coughing, and not bothering even to say good-bye or to shake his horrid hand.

DECEMBER 1900

———

XIII

BATTLE

As soon as she is lying down on his sofa, stroking his soft carpet, the doctor goes on the attack. He asks her to tell him all she remembers about Herr Z. "Are you sure you have told me all? Is there nothing you might have forgotten? Is this scene you have described perhaps only a fragment that hides something else?" he asks.

She pulls the blanket up over her cold feet in her tight boots. Her father is growing impatient with this slow cure. He makes her walk to the doctor's office with only her maid now or sometimes even alone. At breakfast this morning he said, "No carriage for you, young lady, this afternoon. Your doctor's visits are costing enough as it is, without spending it on the horses. And quite frankly I don't see any noticeable improvement in your behavior. What is going on there? Are you listening to the doctor, his advice? What is he telling you?"

And when she would make no response he said, "You are as surly as ever with both me and your poor mother. Have you no respect for your elders! All I hear from you is the banging of doors!"

The doctor has told her she can choose her subject, but he directs her to return to *his* favorite one, not her father or her mother but Herr Z. He seems to want her to talk about him all the time. She would like to ask him if it is not *he* who is in love with him, not her. Perhaps he is still his patient and is telling him stories about her? Or could Pippina actually be the one? She who was so often ill, after all.

Perhaps he knows them both socially. He seems to know so many of his patients socially. Sometimes he dines with them or visits their country estates, her father has told her. Often he sees them twice a day. After all they are such a small circle of people who stay together in this city, shunned, ulti-mately, despite their knowledge or wealth, by the rest of "good" Viennese society. When she says she cannot think of anything else to tell him about Herr Z, which is not true, he says, "Are you certain you have been entirely truthful? Are you sure you were not once in love with him? That you might not want to admit to this or have repressed this feeling? Are you quite sure? You admit that he took notice of you, that he gave you presents, wrote to you. Was that not at least flatter-ing to a young girl?"

She shakes her head. Vehemently she says, "No! No! *No!*"

She feels they are engaged in a lethal battle in this crowded room. All his old statuettes seem lined up to stare at her disap-provingly like soldiers in an army about to advance on her, to march into battle against her, to mow her down! She is not at all certain this doctor wishes her well, that he feels benevolently or even objectively about her. She senses rather that back there in his corner he is plotting and planning his strategy, her enemy, contemplating his next move, that they are fighting to the death, and he is winning. Yet each day she wakes and feels drawn to walk down the street to his consulting rooms. Something draws her back here almost despite herself.

Yet all of this seems to her not to be about sex or repression at all, as he maintains it is—what he insists on calling her repressed sexual longing for Herr Z., or for her father, or even for him—but rather about power, a struggle for power. And she wants to win! What he wants, it seems to her, is to be right, as people so often do when they argue, no matter what they are arguing about, and this man is particularly persuasive. He is closing in on her with his superior knowledge of life, his experience with sick people, his certitude, his masculine pride. The image that comes back in the dim light of the winter afternoon is of a man's private part, something hard and large, a stone, a flint, a weapon thrusting against his pants. He seems so sure that any healthy girl would desire any man who approaches her. Yet she has no desire for this frightening image. On the contrary. If one applies his logic, one might wonder whether it is not he who desires any girl who approaches him, she cannot help thinking.

She says, "I don't remember ever having had amorous feelings for him." She decides to tell him the truth even if it will offend him. She says, "For goodness' sake, he was too old! He is as old as you! I thought of him more like an uncle, like my uncle Karl, Father's brother. I do not like old men in the way you suggest." She senses in the silence that follows the offense she has given. So she says, trying to please him, "I did have a friend who once accused me of being wild about him. But I don't remember that, and certainly, after he had thrust himself at me, I was repulsed by him. Surely you understand that!" she says. She was only thirteen and the daughter of his friend—a friend who was his wife's lover.

"I'm not sure that the age or even the situation is so important here. A thirteen-year-old girl is quite capable of feeling desire, is she not? After all, your mother was betrothed, I seem to remember you saying, at seventeen."

"You have a good memory for facts that are useful to you," she says angrily.

He laughs a little at that. He says it is not as good as it used to be when he was very young and had a photographic memory that enabled him to pass his medical exams quite easily. "Even very young children have strong desires, after all," the doctor says quite reasonably.

"It is true I loved Father passionately as a child; I would have given my life for him, and that is why I am so angry with him now," she says. But then, she surprises herself with her own words. She says, "If you really do want to hear the truth, as you keep saying you do, the person I was really in love with at that time, really in love with, was not Herr Z. at all, as you keep insisting, but rather his wife, Pippina"—she says her name with pleasure.

There is silence in the doctor's room after this remark, which rather pleases her. This, he was perhaps not expecting.

Yet she sees Pippina's dark blue eyes, the thick blond hair

worn in soft ringlets around her oval-shaped face, the bright-red kimono with its embroidered flowers that she often wore in her bedroom, the silk clinging to her soft, welcoming body, the gentle way her head tilts a little to one side, like a Renaissance painting of the Madonna, like a Raphael.

She wonders if Pippina has lain on this silky carpet where she lies now, so miserably.

She tells him that when she was fourteen, she had gone on summer holiday alone with the Z.'s to the Austrian Tyrol. It was a simple place in the mountains, a small town, where they had rented a tiny house, but it seemed lovely to her as she was there with Pippina. "Herr Z. was often absent, and Pippina and I were alone with the children, you see. I loved everything about the place: all the little shops because we went shopping there together, the tiny dark wine stores with their straw-covered brick steps, going down into the cellars, even the grocery shops, the fruit stores with the bright fruit piled up outside, the pharmacy where we went to buy Clara's medicine.

"Probably they invited me on my own so that I could help with the children, particularly Clara, who was sick," she tells him.

What drew her at first to Pippina that summer was her tenderness with her own children: she was always teaching the little girl, reading to her in her soft, sweet Italian voice or teaching her to read, or letting the little boy clamber up into her lap to play some game with her. And she loved to watch her sew in the evenings, her little hands moving so cleverly. She would help her sort out the skeins of bright silk, or pick up her scissors if she dropped them, or thread her needle if she had difficulty. All Pippina's movements seemed so elegant, elegant, and also efficient, adroit.

She and Pippina had slept at the top of the house in a room under the eaves, in a double bed together with the children in their cots. Indeed, Clara, who was so often ill, her heart fluttering wildly like a little bird in her chest, trying to escape, she would say, sometimes climbed up and slept between them if she woke in the night. Together they would tend to her, lying beside her in the darkened room, telling stories.

"I would lie there in the half dark. I could see nothing but Pippina's two large, dark eyes. I felt her gaze was penetrating to my very soul. I loved her then without any sort of reservation, despite what I knew was happening with Father and with her husband. Indeed, in some ways I put up with it all, and kept silent, just because of her. I so wanted her to be happy. I loved everything around her. Little Clara would lie with her head in her mother's lap and her legs across my knees, while her mother told her stories, and I felt that my whole body was part of her mother's through the child's body. I wanted to cover the mother's forehead with the shower of kisses I gave the little girl's knees, her little feet, her toes. I longed to dedicate myself to the little sick girl, to make her well, and to the mother, indeed, in a way, to the whole family. I felt I would do anything for her, for them.

"Pippina knows wonderfully strange Italian folk stories, like the one about a half bird half man," she tells the doctor. "She would sing as well in such a sweet voice. She knows lots of the well-known Italian arias from operas like *Don Giovanni* or *Rigoletto. Caro nome*, she would sing, and I would lie in the half dark beside her and listen with such pleasure.

"Sometimes she would weep. I knew she was so unhappy about many things: her child's illness above all, of course, which is serious, and also I knew she was unhappy with her husband, who betrayed her constantly, as he had tried to betray her with me, and that, too, formed a bond between us, a sort of complicity, though we never spoke of it. Sometimes, too, we would play cards together—she is good at card games—such a clever woman who takes an interest in books like I do, just the blue night-light lit, sitting by the bed while Clara slept."

They would play the honeymoon bridge that would one day be so useful to them both and provide a means of making a living.

Herr Z., when he was there, slept alone in a room at the end of the corridor on the pretext that he needed to work, but the truth was, Pippina had banished him from her bed, so as to be free of his unwanted caresses.

"Like Mother with Father, Pippina seemed to have no desire for Hans, who, I suspect, is probably sick like Father. Perhaps you cured him of his disease, too?"

Pippina said she had taken her into her room to help with the children but she understood it was so they could be more intimate, and she was thrilled.

"We would whisper together in the muffled light, lying beside Clara, who would sometimes moan softly in her disturbed sleep, poor little girl. We read so many books together and discussed them—plays like *Romeo and Juliet* or *Midsummer*

Night's Dream, which we read aloud to the children. We would exaggerate and make the children laugh. Or we did *Twelfth Night* with Pippina sometimes playing the pompous Mercurio, and sometimes myself. We read love poetry by Goethe or Novalis," she says.

She came to adore Pippina—"I loved her unconditionally. I wanted to shine for her. I made up fantasies where I saved her from dangerous situations: pirates, shipwrecks, battles, and she thanked me with her kisses. Or I played the piano at some grand and imaginary concert and she applauded loudly. She sat radiant in the audience and came rushing up at the end onto the stage with flowers and kissed me and said, 'That was beautiful!'

"She held my hand in the night and told me I was such a kind, warmhearted, and sensitive child, and she didn't know what she would do without me. Sometimes she called me *"carissima."* She made me laugh, and gave me so many presents: some of the most wonderful big hats and fine dresses that she made herself—I'm wearing one of her dresses today," she tells the doctor, spreading out her skirt on the couch. 'You take it, darling, it looks much better on you,' she would say.

"Once, just once—but I'll never forget it—one night she reached across the bed and took me into her arms and played the lover, holding me close and kissing me, and touching my new breasts," she tells the doctor. "She told me she preferred to be beside me because I was so soft and sweet and gentle, because I was so loving with her little girl, her children, rather than her husband who was brusque and boorish. But, in the end, it was all a sham. *A sham!*" she says.

"One morning I caught a glimpse of Pippina as she came from her bath. She was naked, her beautiful white body shimmering in the sunlight, her hair falling down like a golden rope, as she leaned forward to pick up the towel she had dropped. She did not seem embarrassed at all and took her time.

"When she saw me staring at her she just shrugged and smiled and said, 'Nothing you haven't seen before.' Which wasn't true. I had never seen anything so beautiful. A woman's body is always much more beautiful than a man's, isn't it?" she asks the doctor, who does not deny it.

"We spoke of things I could never have spoken of with Mother, who cares only about the household chores or going to spas with old sick people, and never discussing what is in her heart.

"I opened up my heart to Pippina. I told her my secrets, though I never mentioned what her husband had done to me, as I was afraid that might hurt her. But I told her about the French fräulein and the forbidden books she gave me to read, though I promised I wouldn't, and how I had read Mantegazza's *The Physiology of Love*. We had endless discussions about the ridiculous differences between men and women and how they are viewed here in Viennese society, the way 'decent' women are supposed to cover themselves up even in the bath, and are not even allowed to ride bicycles, while the men are out roaming the streets looking for prostitutes in the shady parts of the town, where they throng half-naked, giving and getting, the poor things, so many awful diseases.

"How *could* she have repeated all these things I had

confided to her in privacy to her husband, so that he could use them against me, with Father. How *could* she have been so false?" she says.

"Another betrayal, eh?" the doctor says.

"Don't you agree Father has betrayed me by bringing me here, so that you'll get me to do what he and Herr Z. want me to?" she asks.

XIV

MISSING FLIESS

HE SITS ALONE IN HIS study after dinner while the rest of the family sleeps. He wonders if it is his book on dreams, which Fliess helped him write, that is the real cause of his drifting away and not the quarrel over bisexuality. Fliess had read all those pages as he wrote them, with such diligence and perception, advising the removal of certain dreams, critiquing the writing in detail in the most helpful way. His encouragement, his critiques, his insight were all essential to him in the process. Fliess's belief in the brilliance of his discoveries enabled him to continue. He could not have written the book without him. Is it possible that such a generous, fine, upstanding man could actually be jealous now that the book is finished and out in the public eye, despite its poor reception? Could this be the cause of his friend's hurtful silence?

He paces back and forth in his dimly lit study smoking his cigar. The night is cold but dry, the air filled with the odor of smoke and dead leaves that lie in the courtyard outside his window. He cannot sleep. He knows Fliess, his *liebster*

Freund, was right about bisexuality—is not this obsession with Fliess himself proof enough? And he knows, too, that it was Fliess who had brought this up first. It was a case where he himself had protested too strongly, scoffing at the idea initially. Afterward he had to acknowledge that Fliess was right. Now his young patient is confirming his friend's theory and the importance of bisexuality in the neuroses.

He remembers their walking tour from Hirschbuhel to Salzburg almost ten years earlier and how close he had felt to him then, how full of admiration. He was aware, even then, that his friend was searching for a subject that would fully engage his original and lively mind. He recalls how tactful, how helpful Fliess had been, when the doctor had experienced an acute attack of train anxiety. How could he go on without him? Is he to lose this friend, too, as he lost Breuer? This would be a worse blow. He was never this close to Breuer.

He would so much like to talk to Fliess about this latest case. The girl seems to be opening up to him completely, and though she has never admitted to feeling desire for Herr Z. or for himself, she may be about to do so. He has to acknowledge there are moments when he finds her most appealing himself.

He stops his pacing. On an impulse, he picks up his hat and his coat from the chair where he left them earlier in the day. He smooths back his thick hair and adjusts his hat in front of the mirror, rearranges his bow tie. Not a bad-looking man, he thinks. Surely not old yet! he thinks and remembers his patient's unkind words about men his age. He has never had a patient this young, beautiful, and brilliant—or this rebellious. Despite the late hour he decides he will go for a walk. The cold air will do him good, the exercise will help him to sleep, perhaps.

He walks fast in the empty, cold street for a while, not looking up, hugging the walls. He walks past his patient's house, glancing up to see if the lights are still lit in the windows, but the family seems to sleep. Suddenly, he hears a loud, high-pitched laugh. In the light of the street lamp he sees an elegantly dressed woman with a painted face, a fox fur around her white neck. She walks toward him on the arm of another woman similarly dressed though obviously not as young. The younger one covers her mouth with a hand when she sees him. The laughing lady glances at him from the corner of her eye, leans toward her companion, and murmurs something incomprehensible, their mocking, rouged faces close.

Expensive whores, the doctor can see, which does not mean that they might not carry disease as the others do, he thinks. He glimpses a flash of white breast, smells a pungent odor of hyacinth before the women turn and disappear into a doorway. He hears the clack of a door with a tilt of his thudding heart.

He walks on, his thoughts reverting to his young, rebellious, and attractive patient. The girl's words ring in his ears: "A woman's body is always much more beautiful than a man's, isn't it?" Though at times he has little sympathy for this spoiled girl, he would be sorry to lose her, he thinks. Very sorry. He is so used to her coming in his door day after day with her strange and interesting story. He waits for her arrival with impatience. Her case preoccupies him, he has to admit, has preoccupied him since his first glimpse of her: he has entered into her concerns, he is aware, understood her stratagems, and gone ahead of her in her tale of woe, glimpsing clearly the underpinnings. He almost knows what she will say before she says it in the strangest way. He thinks about her more than he should. He remembers her father saying, "I have spoiled her, I'm afraid. We grew too close when I was ill. I used her as a confidant, a friend, and not the child she was. And now she is so angry with me. It's breaking my heart." Has the doctor let her grow too close? Would losing her break his heart?

He is both entirely on her side and completely against her. They are engaged in a battle of wills. He understands what she feels, admires her quick mind and plucky spirit, and at the same time is exasperated by her childish, superficial attempts to manipulate men. This girl is trouble and will probably always be trouble, he thinks. He both envies and feels sorry for the man who marries her, if she ever marries. But then who can understand the mysterious life of a woman? And who can entirely understand the life of a man? And how we hold on to our enemies, he thinks. In the end they may preoccupy us, and be closer to us than those we love.

He keeps walking and is out so late that when he comes back into his building the milk wagon already stands before the house, and the maid is there in the dawn light, down on her hands and knees, scrubbing the entrance. He watches the movement of her ample buttocks in her gray skirts as she scrubs. He thinks of his dream of entering a small gate between two marble buildings. He stands there aware that he is aroused.

XV

AT THE LAKE

"IF YOU REALLY WANT TO know everything that happened with Herr Z., as you say you do, I will tell you the whole story," she says this afternoon, coming into his room, walking without any difficulty, her voice clear, and almost throwing herself down on his couch, "because you *do* seem to be the only one who believes me, or at least you believe me when I tell you what Herr Z. has done. And you do listen to me, at least. Perhaps if I tell you what really happened, you will be on my side and not Father's and get him to leave Frau Z., to banish both of them from his life and my own."

"I'm not so sure that that would be helpful to you. It would only reinforce the idea that being ill makes people do what you want them to do, that you can use illness for your own ends," he says. "But go on, tell me what happened anyway," he adds. "At least it may help you to see it all more clearly."

He does seem ever curious, sitting there so quietly behind her in the shadows of his shadowy room.

She says this happened on a visit to the lovely hotel on Lago di Garda.

"On the same visit when you discovered your father's affair with Frau Z.?" he asks.

"No, no, this was much later. We had gone back there one summer, when I was fifteen. Mother told me to accompany Herr Z. on a walk one afternoon and it was then that he dared to renew his attack. What he didn't know was that I had spoken recently with the fräulein."

"Your French fräulein?" the doctor asks.

"No, no, this was the Austrian one whom the Z.'s had hired that summer, a pretty, redheaded girl with green eyes, and quite young—a simple girl who came from some small town in the mountains. Poor thing, she was obviously in love with Herr Z., just as my own fräulein had been with my father. Herr Z. had even managed to seduce the foolish girl, as he was trying to seduce me, by playing on our sympathies, saying how alone he felt and telling her that he could get nothing from his wife."

She can still see the scene very clearly: sitting down beside him on a bench in the shade. "We had taken the ferry across the lake and then gone walking together on the path along the edge of the water. It was a hot day, and we had stopped so that I could catch my breath." She has difficulty breathing if she walks for any length of time. Perhaps she was also feeling anxious to find herself alone again with Hans.

"At first he rolled a cigarette for me and asked me if I would like to smoke, which I refused, and then he leaned toward me. I could see how red his face had become and how he drew his fingers through his curly dark hair so nervously. He told me that he was so unhappy with his wife. They had become increasingly estranged. Now they slept in separate rooms all the time—as I well knew. He could get nothing from his wife. He actually used *exactly* the same words that he had just used with his fräulein, which unfortunately for him she had confided to me. How little imagination the man has!" she says with disdain, feeling a pain down her right side and her throat closing up as she speaks.

"What else did he say?" the doctor asks.

She wants the doctor to know and manages to speak.

"He said he did nothing but think of me, that he could not get me out of his mind, that he wanted me so desperately, he was willing to leave his wife and start over again with me—and a lot of clichéd statements of that kind that I didn't believe for a minute! His eyes seemed to bulge like a frog's, and I could smell his perspiration, and I wanted to tell him to stop talking about such things. He clutched at my hands, there on the bench in a public place! I was only fifteen! But he held on to me and went on talking about his poor wife, poor Pippina, and how cold and distant she was to him, how lonely marriage could be, how it had all been such a mistake, and it was me he desired and me he wanted to spend his days with.

"That was when I freed my hands and slapped him hard across the cheek. I kept thinking all the time that his trite words were the same ones he had just used with a servant! Who did he think I was?"

"So what you felt was jealousy? And what happened then?" the doctor asks.

She says, "I got up quickly, and I just left him sitting there and rushed home. I wanted to tell Mother what had happened, though he caught up with me on the ferry and begged me not to mention it to my parents."

She had waited a few days to tell them, but this time she did have the courage. She told her father what had happened. But when her father and her uncle questioned Herr Z., he had had the audacity to tell her father she was making it all up, that it was all a figment of her disturbed mind. "He dared to say that it must have come from the texts I had read too young, which had influenced me and given me such unhealthy ideas. He knew that I was reading what he called unsuitable literature because his wife had told him!" she says, waving her hands in the air. "And Father believed him and Pippina rather than me! All Father would say was that I must go with him to see his doctor who would get me to be more reasonable.

"Don't you finally understand that both of us, you and me, are being used by Father in his sordid game? Are you willing to go along with this just because he is paying you? Are you going to just do what Father asks for money like a prostitute?" she asks him angrily.

The doctor says, "I'm not so sure it is as simple as you make it out to be. Could this not have been a serious proposition from Herr Z.?" he asks. "Was it not possible, after all, that he had really fallen in love with you and was really considering leaving his wife to start his life again with someone new, someone young and fresh? Perhaps he really means to marry you one day when you come of age, even if the man may have chosen his words poorly? And would that not be, perhaps, the best solution for all parties involved?"

She sits up and turns to him, coughing. She says angrily, "He would never leave his wife if only because of the children, whom he does really love." She adds, "Would this have been your advice if one of your own daughters had come to you at fifteen after receiving a proposition from a married man?"

He says nothing to that, just turns his face away. She goes on, "If he were really in love with me, if it were true, he would have found some new way to say it surely and not used the words he had just used with a servant!"

As she limps out of his room, pains in her legs, leaving the doctor slumped there unmoving in his chair, she wonders how he can put forth a theory of this kind. Has he perhaps discussed the matter with Herr Z.?

XVI

REVENGE

IT'S ONLY FOUR THIRTY BUT already almost dark when she gets home. The inner courtyard, with its creeper-covered walls, the little fountain in the middle, and the cedar trees is still and dim. Without thinking, she walks along the dark corridor and into the quiet of her father's study. The maids have already drawn the curtains on the encroaching darkness. She lights a lamp. Her brother must be out at the university, or perhaps meeting with his friends, and her mother down in the kitchen supervising the preparations for dinner or chasing after the maids somewhere in the rest of the house. Her father is away on a visit to one of his factories in Bohemia where there has been trouble once again.

There is rarely anyone in this room at this hour of the late afternoon. Indeed, it is a room that is seldom used. She does not risk being disturbed.

She stands, feeling her heart beat fast. Something is about to happen but what, she is not sure. Something has to happen. She hears the slow ticking of her father's green and gold clock on the mantelpiece, the distant, mournful sound of a train's whistle.

She smells her father's cigar smoke in the air. As she looks at the sweep of his large, shiny desk, the silver paper knife glints invitingly against the dark mahogany. She thinks of the young Werther again, in her favorite book.

She unpins her hat, runs her hands through her unruly curls, throws off her coat and lined gloves onto his leather armchair by the window, and stands uncertainly, her fingertips on the desk, trembling a little all over, her legs aching, her throat sore from coughing. As she thinks of the doctor's words—"Perhaps he really means to marry you one day when you come of age, even if the man may have chosen his words poorly? And would that not be, perhaps, the best solution for all parties involved?"—she is coughing again and has a terrible pain down the right side of her stomach and her leg. *What is the point of going on?*

She picks up the paper knife and walks over to the round gold-framed mirror on the wall between the two windows. She looks at the pale face, the dark, wild hair, the large dark eyes, now filled with tears. *Who are you? What will become of you? And who cares?* She looks down at her slim wrist, finds the blue vein, and runs the serrated edge of the knife lightly across it. Then she presses down harder, looking up at her face.

The lines from Goethe's lovely poem come to her:

> *The little birds fall silent in the forest;*
> *Just wait, soon you too shall rest.*

Is this her only way out?

Is it what she really wants, to rest eternally, or is it just to be able to see their faces when they find her resting, lying in a pool of blood on the floor? Would she like to come back to her own funeral to see them weep? What she wants is revenge, revenge on all the adults around her who have failed her again and again—all of them. How *can* she get back at them? How *can* she make them weep? How can she at least get them to pay attention to her suffering heart?

How *can* the doctor imagine that Herr Z. would really leave his lovely wife and small children to marry her? How can he take the hackneyed words Herr Z. used to seduce her seriously, exactly the same ones he had used with his children's governess who had just been seduced? What a gullible man, who sometimes seems so innocent or ignorant to her despite all his fancy learning.

And how could the doctor imagine *she* wants to marry a man the age of her father, an old adulterer, a wrinkled Don Juan, when she has a fresh-faced, dimpled, and innocent young engineering student already in her mind and heart. Why would she choose the old, dull, and gray over the young, shiny, and fresh skinned?

Why should *she* want to marry an old man of the doctor's age? How can he imagine this as a solution? Is it perhaps because he, himself, would like to start his life over with someone young, pretty, and fresh like herself? Is he tired of his wife?

But what other choices does she really have? Is this what her father has in mind for her? Has the doctor promised him to get her to be reasonable, to do as her father wishes? Have they made an agreement of some kind? Is she to be sold to this old lecherous man in exchange for his wife's favors? What can she do? How can she protect herself? Who can she turn to? Who will help?

She stares at the bookcases, with all the bound books, running along one wall behind her father's pompous Empire desk with its dark wood and heavy gold filigree. Her father is not a real reader as she is, and most of the elegant bound volumes with their gold lettering and shiny covers remain untouched except by the maids, who dust them daily, and by her mother who checks daily to see that they have been dusted. It is all just a shiny facade maintained to impress visitors, or perhaps to convince her father, himself, of his culture. All the many volumes of Shakespeare and Milton, of Hegel and Schopenhauer, of Goethe and Schiller—there are even little white china statues of Goethe and Schiller in their frockcoats—are all there for show. Like so much about her father, they are all just a handsome exterior to seduce, to manipulate, to get what he wants from others.

She searches the volumes to see if there is anything that might help her in her battle with the doctor. As she stands there, biting her lips, her breath coming and going irregularly, pains in her legs, she spots a book on a high shelf with a gray cover and the name: Dr. Sigm. Freud. It is his book on dreams, which her father has shelved in an inaccessible place like something prohibited, and thus all the more attractive to her.

She steps up the wooden ladder, stretches up, and takes the

book down. She puts it on the desk and looks at the Latin inscription on the cover, which she puzzles over. Her Latin is not very good. Eventually she makes it out: *Flectere si nequeo superos*—If I cannot move heaven—*acheronta movebo*—I will raise hell. A clever motto for a book. She would like to raise hell. She must write it down in her diary on the title page. She opens the book and sees it is an inscribed copy made out to her father, who has clearly not read it, the pages new and crisp.

She takes the book to her room, shuts her door, pulls out her own diary, and places them side by side on her desk. She will take some notes. Her father is not likely to miss the doctor's book, and surely the information she may glean here will increase her arsenal in this battle with these men and women, all the adults who have betrayed her, who have refused to see the reality around them. She sits down in the pale, chintz-covered armchair in the quiet of the late winter afternoon, puts a tasseled gray shawl around her shoulders, and reads.

The doctor often asks her about her dreams, and she is curious as to what he might do with one if she were to offer him something to keep him happy for a while. Would that please him and perhaps even distract him from his goal of preparing her to accept Herr Z. and his marriage proposal? Perhaps she can get him to concentrate on her dreams while she thinks what to do, how to escape her predicament.

She turns the pages, taking the voyage he seems to suggest the reader must take with him, though she does not take all the detours. She does not bother much with the first chapters, which she finds boring, a history of what people have said about dreams before the doctor. She does not always understand the complicated twists and turns of the doctor's mind or bother with some of his intricate reasoning. She becomes interested only when she comes upon his own dreams, where she finds out something about *him*. Some of the dreams he gives as the dreams of other patients she suspects are his own. She wants to know *his* secrets, and he certainly seems to share some here! She wants to know everything she can about him, his family, his wife, his children.

He writes about the death of his father, which has apparently been such an important event in his life. He writes about his longing to go to Rome and his dreams about the city. She likes the parts about his travels to Italy, which he admires and where he has found some of the things in his office. She likes the children's dreams and particularly the one his own small daughter, deprived of food after an illness, has, calling out in the night a list of desired foods including "stwawbewwies," which makes her laugh.

Even more interesting is the more complicated one about an injection and a patient called Irma. It interests her as the doctor seems to feel guilty about something he has done to one of his patients or perhaps to someone else. There is even one where she understands the doctor dreams of embracing his daughter! She understands that the doctor believes that all dreams, even nightmares, are disguised wishes and she finds the part about how they are disguised interesting, like a political writer who has to avoid the censorship of the government. She understands what he means by that because of her brother and the pamphlets he writes.

It occurs to her that she could take the doctor a dream. Since she has been seeing the doctor, she does indeed dream more, and even the sorts of dreams he likes to interpret, as though her unconscious were trying to provide what he needs. She does not mind dreaming for him, but her dreams seem small, vague things, compared to his, which are often lengthy and detailed with several people and dialogue. She is afraid her dreams would not be good enough. She rarely remembers a complete dream, and when she does it seems sketchy and without the kind of specific detail that she finds in the doctor's dreams or the dreams of his patients. There is rarely any talking in her dreams; hardly ever any *words* in her dreams, or if they occur they are written in large letters she can read. Her dreams, like her early memories, are in pictures without much dialogue. She sees them. The only place she makes up dialogue is in her fantasy where the fräulein asks the little boy what he has been doing and if he is a good boy.

But she could make a dream up for the doctor, she thinks, sitting at her desk and paging through his book, reading here and there. She does not think it would be too difficult to invent one or two to suit him now that she has read some of his own and knows how he interprets them.

It is not that hard to figure it out: one thing stands in for another, she understands: a flag as an example of the fatherland; but objects in the dreams the doctor reports are almost always symbols of sexual things: a jewel and particularly a jewel box are a woman's private parts, and anything longer than it is wide, like the pen that lies on her desk by her diary with its oozing ink, is a man's. A hat is interpreted, making her laugh, as a man's part, and indeed, thinking of the way her father wears hats she thinks he might be right. Every time a train enters a tunnel or a key a lock it is quite obvious what the doctor would think, that poor frustrated man.

Also, he considers every strongly expressed opinion actually means the opposite. Of course, he is not entirely wrong about that, either. It is a topsy-turvy world: fire is water; death is life; horror means attraction; hate is love.

Leafing through the book before her, she cannot help feeling both admiration and a kind of sympathy for its author. She finds that the voice in the book is both credible and persuasive. He writes remarkably well, she must admit. Obviously the doctor struggles just as she does to find the meaning of things. She understands from this book that he has several children—perhaps too many, and a wife who may not be much more giving than her own mother, a pale, reserved woman, she gathers from a dream, who would prefer not to be penetrated from behind.

Naturally, the poor women do not want to have trains in their tunnels, if it means producing yet another child, which might either kill them or cause them to contract some horrible sexual disease, and will at least cause them to become even more overworked. Like someone deprived of food who can think of nothing else, the doctor thinks about sexual things all the time, perhaps, because he lacks them, she imagines.

She realizes that she feels two completely contradictory things: she is in a rage with him, but at the same time the thought of leaving him makes her feel almost physically ill. She realizes that talking to him every day, telling him so much of her story, she has grown dependent on him, attached to him, if only as a means to leave her own house, her own parents, to have someone who is entirely at her disposal for an hour. Despite herself and despite his sometimes infuriating responses, she would like to please him by giving him some support for his theories, or as her French fräulein would say: "*de l'eau pour son moulin.*" He is obviously trying so very hard to earn a living as best he can. An ambitious man, an intellectual *parvenu*, he would like to be a professor, she understands from his text. He listens and observes very carefully. He notices things other people either ignore or deny, like gestures. He once said something wonderful about her fingers chattering. He is certainly right about the hypocrisy and humbug of most people in Viennese society, including her own family. She likes his desire to see clearly into the human heart and mind, to delve for the truth, and she has become aware of things she did not know in the process of talking to him. She likes his ability to cut through the cant and hypocrisy of the people who surround her.

She finds him remarkably clever and even convincing in certain ways. He follows his outrageous ideas quite courageously to their logical conclusions, though she does not think his observations are always correct or could possibly cure her. Certainly he is not afraid of what people will say and think! He is a brave man, unlike her father or even her brother, who so often lie and take the easy way out.

The doctor thinks her constant cough comes from her identification with Frau Z., whom he imagines performs fellatio on her father. What a ghastly and embarrassing thought!

He doesn't know that her fantasies about Frau Z. are really of stroking her private parts and putting her tongue in there, which might provide much more pleasure than her father does! The very thought makes her start to cough.

She will try to come up with a dream that will please him and distract him at least for a while. She looks around her room with its pale walls, the bed pushed against the wall, the bowl of dried flowers on the desk, the little pink lamp with its tassels by the bed. How much she has suffered and hoped in silence between these walls. She will try and imitate the dreams from his book. She will use the compression, displacement, and condensation he speaks of; she will intensify the ideas. She takes out her pen and copies the inscription in his book into her diary. Then she tries out a few dreams in its pages, attempting to make them sound just like the ones in the dream book, writing them in a voice that resembles the doctor's and using exact details and conversation, which she doesn't usually hear or anyway remember in her own dreams, but which seem to come up frequently in the doctor's dreams and those of his patients, he reports. She imagines how he would interpret them and decides on two which she likes particularly. She decides to start with one, which is short and simple, and see his reaction and if she gets away with her ruse. Then she will take him a second one which is longer and rather more complicated.

XVII

THE FIRST DREAM

SHE BRINGS THE DOCTOR THE first one. She is rather proud of it, though she is a little nervous that he might deduce her duplicity. She has kept this first one quite short and fairly simple and used bits and pieces of dreams she has really dreamed. She has added a line of dialogue and the images she knows the doctor will recognize. She has provided all the necessary elements: her father, her mother, her brother, a fire, and, of course, a jewel box which needs to be saved from the fire. The doctor, she has remarked, seems particularly interested in boxes of one kind or another, and she knows how he will interpret this one.

"I have a dream for you," she says in a clear voice.

"Ah, excellent! Tell me what you dreamed," he responds.

There is a fire in the house. Father stands before my bed and awakens me. I dress myself quickly. Mama still wants to save her jewelry box, but Papa says, "I do not want my children and me to burn up because of your jewelry box." We hurry down, and as soon as I am outside I wake up.

"That's it?' he asks, and she nods.

"And when did you dream this?" he asks.

For a moment she is taken aback by the question, but she knows he likes to interpret numbers, and seems indeed to give them considerable significance, so she quickly says she has dreamed this three times, which doesn't quite answer the question. Three is always such a good number: there are always three princesses or three princes in all the fairy tales.

The doctor, indeed, as she had expected, seems very excited by the dream. He does not question it for a minute but seems to swallow it whole, hook, line, and sinker. What a gullible man, she thinks, ready to believe whatever she says, and feels a little guilty. For a while he stops talking about Herr Z., her desire for him, and a possible marriage to him, as he encourages her to associate freely on the dream.

She would so like to please him, and she is aware she has been rude and disagreeable at times. She imagines he thinks of her as *recalcitrant*, a word he uses in his dream book to describe several of his patients who resist his interpretations. She feels she has wounded his self-esteem in a way. Perhaps this dream gift will really help restore his confidence in his work, and advance his career. This will be her gift.

She tells him quite truthfully how her imaginary dream reminds her of the moment Herr Z. came into her hotel room in the afternoon, after his proposal on the lake. She was lying down and taking a nap, and he gave her such a fright. She had, in reality, asked for the key to the room, so that she could make sure he did not disturb her again. She was particularly afraid he might enter the room when she was undressing and see her naked.

The doctor interprets the dream at some length, showing off a bit, like a little boy riding a bicycle with no hands. He says the escape from the house represents her wish to escape from *him* and leave the treatment, which is not so far off the mark. She thinks that this dream story does indeed express her fears in a way. She feels they are, indeed, all in danger, that their existence is precarious at best. She remembers the very real burning of her father's textile factory a few years ago in Bohemia, something the doctor doesn't seem to consider at all, or the recent trouble in the factories because of her father's religion. She is glad her gift has enabled him to come up with all sorts of ingenious interpretations. He puzzles over every aspect of the dream and even writes it down. For the first time she can hear him writing down her exact words, and she is pleased.

When the doctor jumps to the inevitable conclusion, that the jewel box in the dream represents her lady parts, she cannot help saying, "I *knew* you would say that."

"Because you know it's true, don't you? And what do you think about the smoke from the fire?"

XVIII

WOMEN

THE DOCTOR SITS IN HIS study thinking about the dream the girl has brought him and how he can use it. A useful dream, he can see. She has, like so many of his intelligent and wealthy female patients, brought him what he needs to demonstrate his theories.

He intends to use what he has learned from her in this analysis of the dream for his own purposes. Women's sorcery, he realizes, as he looks around his cluttered room with all its ancient statues, need not always be destructive but can be used for his own purposes. He can use his understanding of this clever, attractive young woman, his ability to identify with her. He can use his own feminine side. He can write it down, write it up, analyze it, control it.

It is through the use of women that he, like the hero of Maupassant's *Bel ami*, must advance, he understands. He has already used their early memories, their frank talk, their access to their feelings, which have helped him to understand his own sometimes incomprehensible desires. Women and the great writers, who know all and surely have access to their repressed longings, their bisexuality, and particularly the Greeks with Sophocles and the English with Shakespeare, have said it all before him. Now he must take charge of what they have discovered. He decides that he *will* go to Rome, finally. His fears of contracting some sort of illness there are absurd. He will thrust his hand into the *Bocca della verita*. He will overcome his ambivalence and, unlike Hannibal, storm the gates, and once he has accomplished this, he will write to his influential patient who has repeatedly offered to use her connections in order to obtain his professorship. He has been passive for far too long and put himself through too much suffering. He has, like everyone, a feminine side, feminine intuition, feminine wiles, and it is time to stop denying it and to use it. He will take the path that others have taken for the sake of his career, his ambition, the well-being of his family, his faithful wife. He will scheme. He will plot and plan. He will use his connections, this influential woman and her husband and perhaps even her wealthy friend who has also offered to help. Given the situation, rejected again and again and often enough because of his religion, he must use every means at his disposal. He is tired of being poor and underestimated, passed over again and again for a position he deserves. He needs to take his destiny into his own hands. No one else will do it for him, he realizes. He will write to Elise Gomperz and ask her to use her connections, her money, her friend's paintings, whatever she has in hand.

When he climbs into the conjugal bed that night he reaches over to Martha and wakens her with a caress. He turns her over, and enters her body from behind, and touches her until he hears her moan with pleasure.

XIX

THE SECOND DREAM

CARRIED AWAY BY HER SUCCESS with the first dream, she brings him the second one, which is longer and more complex. She would never have dreamed something this long and remembered it in such detail, but the doctor's dreams are lengthy and filled with details he seems to have remembered. The last dream she read in the dream book is about his mother's death, a dream which has made an impression on her with its beaked figures hovering over the body of the mother. It has given her the idea. Also, the doctor often talks about stations and trains, indeed, he has used the analogy of a train trip to describe an analysis: the first stage being the preparation for the trip, the acquisition of tickets, the planning of the route, and the second stage the actual voyage from one station to the next.

Again she hears him writing down her words:

I go walking in a city that I do not know, and see streets and squares that are foreign to me. Then I come to the house where I live, go into my room, and find lying there a letter from my mother. She writes that since I have been away from home without my parents' knowledge, she has not wanted to tell me that Papa has fallen ill. Now he has died, and if I want to I can come. Then I walk to the station and ask, perhaps one hundred times, Where is the station? I always receive the answer: five minutes. Then I see a thick forest before me into which I enter, and question a man whom I encounter there. He tells me: another two and a half hours. He offers to accompany me. I decline and go on by myself. I see the station in front of me but cannot reach it. This is accompanied by the usual feeling of anxiety that arises in dreams when one cannot move ahead. Then I am home again, which I must have walked to, but I do not know anything more about it. I enter the porter's lodge and ask him about our dwelling. The servant girl opens up for me and answers: Mama and the others are already at the cemetery.

She can really see this city in her imagination in the mist and the gray. She has seen it in a postcard her beloved sent her of a city in Hungary. The letter, of course, is a recall of the letter she wrote announcing her own intention to commit suicide, which she knows the doctor will recognize. Now it is her father who is dead in the dream. This will puzzle the doctor, surely, though he may think of this as her revenge on her father. The doctor likes to make analogies and link things together, she has learned, just as one does in a poem.

Indeed, he interprets the dream with glee, coming up with all sorts of convoluted and complicated reasons for the events, working on it diligently, almost as if she were not there lying before him on his couch, clutching her reticule, with her suffering body, her pains in the legs, her cough coming and going. He asks her for added information, and she speaks of looking up the symptoms of appendicitis in the encyclopedia.

"I like to look up things in the encyclopedia, to find the causes," she tells him and thinks she has used his own book rather like an encyclopedia to look up the meaning of dreams. He has never complimented her on her curiosity or her ambition to learn the meaning of things, but surely that is what makes life interesting: the process of learning. She says that she had suffered from an attack of this kind, which several doctors felt might be the cause of her fever, the pains in her abdomen and down her right leg, and so she wanted to find out what it might be.

"When did this occur?" he naturally wants to know.

She doesn't remember exactly but says this happened nine months after the scene at the lake with Herr Z., which makes him talk about an imaginary pregnancy and not the pains in her stomach or legs or an appendicitis.

"You seem to accuse me of being in love with everyone! So many people: my father, Herr Z., and perhaps even with you! It is very confusing to me. In the meantime I am still suffering from pains in my stomach and my leg, and I keep coughing and feeling as though I will not be able to breathe!" she says, but he doesn't seem to pay attention to that.

It is her dreams that interest him above all and not her pains, she thinks, and certainly not *her*: one suffering girl. It occurs to her that if she were simply to turn into smoke, to rise up on his magic carpet and fly out of the room or become invisible and drift out the window, float out into his courtyard, he might not notice. He might just go on talking, making clever remarks, playing with her words almost as if they were a poem and this a literature class. He is much more interested in this dream, these images she has imagined, than in her real suffering.

How little sympathy he seems to have for a fellow human being. He is interested in a theory he wishes to prove—an imaginary pregnancy, which will prove her desire for Herr Z., which she has supposedly repressed, or her original desire for her father—much more than he is in the suffering of the dreamer, she realizes, with a little shock. He is looking for added information to prove his theories in the dream book, she supposes. It is an intellectual game for him, where he is on a treasure hunt for the gold he hopes will prove his theories and make him famous. She is not sure that he is particularly interested in making her, just one insignificant girl, well or happy. Perhaps he does not really think it is possible, though he said he did, and perhaps he is right. Perhaps it is impossible to be without pain of some kind, without suffering. But she also feels he is talking more about his own life than hers.

She wonders how she could get him to concentrate on her and what she is thinking and feeling. How can she reach him? How can she get him to pay attention to *her*? What weapons does she have at her disposal? She wonders what he would say if she were simply to tell him that she has decided to end the treatment, to leave. Would he then become aware of her suffering presence? Would he say he would miss her? Would he beg her to stay? Or at least advise her to continue her treatment in order to get well? Would he at least miss the money her father is paying him? How can she get a rise out of him, get him to react in some way to her real life, to *her, to her*?

Would he even say that he needs more time to cure her of her ills? For a mad moment she imagines the doctor down on his knees, his hands lifted in prayer, his male member thrusting in supplication against his trousers.

Suddenly she needs to know. She determines to tell him at the start of the next session, at the start of the year, that she is leaving, and to see what happens. Surely then he will pay attention to *her*, take her words more seriously and beg her to stay. In the meantime she will change the subject slightly and tell him about a painting that intrigued her.

XX

THE MADONNA

HE GLANCES AT THE CLOCK, but there are still some minutes left until the end of the session. The girl is talking about something she did recently: sitting for two hours in the art gallery in Dresden looking at a painting of the virgin by Raphael, the *Sistine Madonna*.

He remembers the train ride to Dresden and the altercation with a rude Christian who had called him a dirty Jew when he wanted to open a window. The man had insisted he close the window, and now this girl is going on about the Madonna in the museum in Dresden. He remembers the painting, which he saw so long ago—it must be seventeen years, he thinks, the span of this girl's life. How madly he had been in love with his princess at the time.

But he asks her, "And why did you sit there so long? Two hours is a long time! What was so interesting about the painting?"

"I'm not certain," she says.

"Which part of the picture interested you particularly?"

he asks, thinking of the central figure of the Madonna and
the baby and the couple that flank them: on one side an older
man, if he remembers correctly, some saint, or pope most
probably, who points a finger at the viewer but looks up at the
baby, and on the other side a beautiful blond woman with a
mysteriously lowered gaze.

"The Madonna," she says and adds, "I didn't understand
what Raphael was trying to say in this painting."

"You think he was trying to say something?" he asks.

"The Madonna looks so frightened, as though she has
seen something awful. She seemed to me to be trying to escape, to run forward, to run out of the picture, to run away
from something."

"What made you think she was running, escaping?" the
doctor asks.

"You can see by her skirts moving around her ankles and
the position of her feet," she says. "Also, the baby Jesus seemed
so strange to me, not at all the way he is usually portrayed. I
was so puzzled by his expression. Have you seen the painting?
Do you know what I mean?" she asks.

He admits that he has seen the painting but it was a long
time ago, and adds, "That's not what I remember," and thinks
that he was more interested in the Madonna. "What was so
strange about the Christ child?" he asks.

"I thought he looked angry, or perhaps afraid, rather the
way I have felt at times: his eyes stare so fearfully, and his hair
is all in a mess, and his teeth seemed clenched with horror. I
thought he looked as if he had seen some dreadful apparition,
or anyway the way I felt when I had awoken and found Herr

Z. by my bed, and how I felt when he suddenly clattered down the steps at his shop and clutched me to his chest."

"I must have missed that during my brief inspection," he says and remembers that the Madonna had actually reminded him of a young nursemaid and not any heavenly creature at all.

She says, "I felt the Madonna might be considering what was about to happen in the future to her baby, or perhaps even to all of us, and would have wanted to escape it. Only the beautiful woman on the right who looks down seems not to know or not to want to know what is about to happen to everyone. And the two little adorable angels at the bottom of the painting seem to be looking on ironically or with even a touch of humor. I somehow felt the painting was trying to warn me of something."

"And what could that be?" the doctor asks her.

"I don't know," she tells him, shaking her head.

"It is certainly a beautiful painting of the Madonna," the doctor now admits, though he is thinking of his own increasing isolation within Christian society and how he has been driven back to his own people, joining B'nai B'rith, where he has found some comfort and companionship.

She tells the doctor that she was drawn to the painting because it seemed directed at her. She felt an intimate part of the family portrayed there. "In a way I felt I was both the Madonna and the baby, and also the little angels watching the scene. It was an awful feeling. I felt the older man was both like my father and Herr Z. and perhaps, come to think of it now, also like you, all of you pointing the way I am supposed to go, urging me to do your bidding, none of you really thinking of what might be best for me in the end. The beautiful woman was both Mother, who refuses to lift her eyes and see how terrible it all is, and the blond, beautiful, and mysterious Pippina, who insists on ignoring the horror of my real situation and her own."

"And you felt no longing to be like the Madonna, to one day bear a child, a baby yourself?" he finds himself saying, thinking of his own children and how he loves them, and how much pleasure they have given him with their amusing, charming ways. He thinks of young Martin, who already shows such promise with his imaginative poems; such an intelligent child, a strange bird, sensitive and good natured.

She says, "I have no wish to marry and bear children. What happiness have men brought me? What have they ever given me? How have they ever helped me?"

He is not sure how to answer her, taken aback by her bitter words. Has he then brought her nothing at all? Have all his words been in vain? Has she gained nothing from her time with him? He looks at the clock and sees it is time for the end of the session.

But later, when she is gone, has left him for good, he will think of what she was trying to tell him. He will think of that painting and her words when he hears, two years later, that she has married despite her bitter words, and to a young engineer apparently of not particularly promising qualities, whom her father has been obliged to take into his employ as he has no other work.

He thinks of the painting again above all, two years after

the marriage, when he hears that she and her husband have had a baby boy and have decided to convert to Lutheranism. Like so many in Viennese Jewish society, he presumes, they hope thus to make it easier for their boy to advance in life, to protect him from the dangers around him, from any danger that might arise. A vain hope, as he will eventually find out, as under the Nazi Nuremberg Laws of 1935 one Jewish grand-parent is enough to condemn a man or woman to death.

XXI

THE LAST SESSION

SHE STARTS THE SESSION BY telling him she has decided this will be the last time she comes to see him. She says she has been determined to stick it out until the end of the year but now she must leave.

She waits to hear what he will say, expecting him to protest, to tell her she is making a great mistake, that this is not what she really wants, that on the contrary she wants to stay, but to her surprise he says nothing. Why does he not respond to her words as he usually does, telling her she is mistaken, that a desire to leave is really her way of getting him to beg her to stay? Surely he understands that? Is he going to remain silent even under these circumstances? What has she done?

"For how long have you been considering this seriously?" is all he asks. Again he wants precise numbers. What is this mania for numbers?

"For two weeks," she answers, though the truth is probably that she has thought of it from time to time since she first set foot in this room, this ultimate plea, an attempt to get him to react, to notice her, to ask her to stay. As she says these words, she is overcome by a pang of regret. Is he just going to let her go without protest? How could she really leave this man she has been talking to every day except Sundays for the last three months? Her intention was simply to get him to respond to her, to tell her he wanted her to stay.

At least he has listened to her with much interest. At least he has believed what she had to say with a trustfulness that is touching. What will she do without him? What will become of her without him? How could she live without coming here every day and without him telling her what her thoughts, her feelings, her dreams mean? Who will she be on her own without having him to confirm or deny her thoughts and feelings? How could she walk out of his door and never come back?

"You are dismissing me like a maid with two weeks' notice?" he says.

There is a moment of stunned silence in the small room that makes her very sad. It is true that this man has listened to her so carefully and paid more attention to her words than anyone else has ever done in her whole life. He has also admitted that what she told him was true, which her father and Herr Z. have not done. It is also true he has bullied her and hectored her and tried to make her admit to his theories and ideas about sexuality. At times she has felt she was under a police investigation, held here under close scrutiny for committing a monstrous crime of some kind. He has accused her of making herself ill by her thumb-sucking and masturbating, of using her illness for her own ends, to manipulate her father, who would do anything for her. He feels the best solution for everyone would be for her to marry Herr Z. What sort of a solution is that?

She tells him that she is very thankful for his help and admits she has found the analysis interesting, though disturbing.

"I have discovered a new way to look at the world, and though I don't always like what I see, I feel more, well, more intelligent, in a way, just from the looking, the possibilities," she says. She doesn't feel much better physically, she must admit, and certainly she is still in a rage with her father and Herr Z., but perhaps she will now have the courage to confront the Z.'s.

The doctor says nothing to all of this. He says nothing about his feelings for her as a human being, as a young girl struggling with what is surely a difficult situation, or even offers any advice about the wisdom of such a decision. He voices not a word of affection or even any interest in the results of her departure. He does not even ask her to stay in touch, to let him know how she is getting on. Instead, he is obviously thinking about himself. He sounds very cross, and repeats something about her treating him like a servant, giving him two weeks' notice.

She understands he has taken her decision personally, and now she does not know what to say. She has offended him. Like a rejected lover, like a child, he is hurt and angry with her and is now sulking in his corner in silence. Well, let him sulk. He is taking her decision to leave as her revenge on him. Perhaps he is not entirely wrong. Perhaps leaving him is the best thing she can do.

Obviously he feels she is rejecting him personally by breaking off the treatment. Perhaps he feels she is breaking off his masculine part which he seems so proud of and of which he speaks so often. She sees the gray stone crumbling. He goes on stubbornly with the analysis of the last dream.

She tries to change the subject and to talk about something else, hoping he might still ask her to stay. She has a little time left, she realizes, looking at his clock, and at least he won't make her leave until her time is up today. What can she say? She had so hoped he would try to convince her to stay, that he might at least point out the advantages of his cure.

When it is time for the end of the session, he simply tells her the time is up. She rises and comes over to him and shakes his hand. She looks into his eyes with real affection and feels the tears rush into her eyes.

"I am so sorry I have to leave like this, but I feel I have no other choice now. I will be back to see you, one day, I'm sure," she says, lifting her voice hopefully while he continues to scowl at her. Awkwardly, she pushes her hat back from her forehead and says she is so sorry that they could not have helped each other more. "I tried," she says. He looks at her and says, coolly, "And can you be so sure we did not?"

JANUARY 1901

XXII

WRITING IT UP

HE SITS IN HIS STUDY, writing up the case all through the cold January nights of the new year. He smokes one cigar after another. He cannot work without this aid, which will one day be his undoing. The cancer of the palate, the operations, the prosthesis, and ultimately the morphine-induced death are all years ahead of him. Surrounded by his prized objects and warmed by the fire burning in the stove, he writes fast and furiously until late. He struggles to get the whole thing down but finally decides to curtail his account, leaving out the analytic process.

For the most part, he follows the slow, uneven process of the girl's own gradual and reluctant revelations and his own penetrating interpretation of them. He models this account on his patient's revelations, withholding certain important facts, until toward the end, just as the girl herself has done.

He realizes that each case presents a mystery story of sorts, perhaps the whole psychoanalytic method is somewhat like a mystery story, a crime novel, a thriller, gradually revealing connections between events and symptoms.

He has read a great deal of fiction in many languages and knows how to tell a story, hinting from the start at what is up ahead, releasing the information little by little, so as to pique the interest of the reader and catch him in his net, as he had hoped to catch this girl. Now he will pin her down with his pen like a butterfly on the page for posterity. He provides many mysterious footnotes to keep his reader questioning the exact reason for the girl's symptoms, her distress.

This will be a necessary compliment to his dream book, supplementing and illustrating his theories with this very real experience. They have criticized him for not providing sufficient clinical illustrations—well, he will provide them with more than they may want.

His wife reproaches him in the morning at breakfast and tells him he looks pale and has dark rings under his eyes. He will make himself ill working this hard, she complains, but he feels driven to get his vision of this girl down on the page.

The father comes several times to say the girl will return, but she comes no more. She has broken off the treatment. She has escaped him, and perhaps the father, too, who seems unable to coerce her into coming back, depriving him of a considerable source of income if nothing else. The case is closed, as far as he is concerned. He will never take her back, should she wish to come. She has treated him shabbily, the way she felt Herr Z. had treated her, using the same words to woo her that he had used with the fräulein. He will use his words to put her in her place on the page.

But as he writes up the case he is increasingly aware that he has failed this girl. As he writes, he realizes what he should have been aware of earlier. Like the other hysterical women he has treated, she has taught him a lot, and not only about the psychoanalytic process, but also about himself. Women, despite his fear of them, his inability to understand them fully, have helped him enormously with his work, he knows. Without their frank words, their ability to understand their own feelings, their capacity for insight, without their connections in the real world, he could never have invented his method, his theories, and spread them. With sadness for her but gladness for him, he realizes that what he has learned from the girl has come too late for her but not for him.

Why had he not seen the break coming and analyzed the transference in time: the girl's obvious anger and fear of him, along with the growing attraction? Why had he not connected these feelings to the obvious echoes from her past, her experiences with her father and above all with Herr Z., which have distorted her image of himself, just as he has distorted the image of his beloved Other, Fliess? He realizes that he has acted like a woman with Fliess, a womanly womb waiting for the intellectual siring of the Other, and it has taken this girl for him to see it, to understand the transference fully.

He is aware in the late-night silence of the street, in his loneliness and loss, that he has overvalued the competence of this man as friend, doctor, and man of science. He has played the woman, the nursemaid to him and his dubious ideas. He has been complicit in his doubtful number games, his wild ideas. He has followed the germination of his preoccupations;

he has encouraged, admired, and adored. He has even tried to help him prove his mad ideas. All of this—Fliess's perplexing biomedical numbers game, the extreme importance given to the nose, and above all his insistence that periods of euphoria inevitably followed periods of melancholy—all suggested that patients became better or worse strictly according to biological periods, whatever one did in an analysis, and this would entirely negate his own work.

He knows he is already envied for the sort of patients who come to him, often wealthy members of his own race. Perhaps Fliess himself is among those who envy him for his discoveries, as indeed so many do his entire race, envy them the ability to get up earlier and work later into the night, envy him this feminine ability to listen to the language of the heart.

He turns back to the text he is writing, determined to use this account to further the progress of psychoanalysis, to further his own position, even if his knowledge has come too late for this girl, even if he has not been able to help her as he would have wished.

Finally he adds a postscript with his later discoveries, comments on the transference, and ideas that have come to him since the girl's departure.

In the preface, which he composes only at the end, when he has the whole case down, he provides his motives for divulging what will be the most intimate and scabrous details of her young life.

He gets it all down in three weeks, and when he has finished, he reads it over with some satisfaction. It is one of the most subtle things he has written, and surely subtlety is the essence of what distinguishes good work from the mediocre. He dares anyone, even a casual observer, to pick up this report and put it down without reading it to the end. It is as good as a short story by one of the great masters.

Yet as he looks around his cluttered study, with all his precious carpets and objects, he finds it empty: something is now missing in his life.

When he steps over to the window, he can see the snow still falling, joining the slush of melting flakes on the ground. He hears water drip from the drainage spout into the courtyard, and the lonely cry of a city bird.

He is moved to take up his pen and write yet another letter to Fliess, one more attempt to reach him, one of his last, though he knows now with a deep sense of loss that his friend, too, like the young girl, will come no more into his life. This man, his Other, whose praise was once nectar and ambrosia to him, has retreated. He is gone, vanished, only a dream of his own mind. He knows now that he existed only in the distortion of his own imagination, that he has endowed him, as one must the loved object, with attributes he never possessed. He will have to go forward without him. He knows he owes him for emphasizing the fact of bisexuality, which the girl has so clearly demonstrated. Yet he feels at this moment short of a drug, certain his friend will understand what he means. He cannot admit that without his approval, he is reluctant to publish this material. Nor does he yet know that he will keep this account to himself for five long years.

APRIL 1, 1902

XXIII

RETURN

SHE WALKS THE SHORT DISTANCE to his consulting rooms on
her own this time. She remembers the first time she went to
the doctor's office, that autumn day, dragged there by her father in the carriage, so full of rage and humiliation. She remembers the pain all through her body. The pain in her leg
has gone, her bowels are regular, her voice clear, though she
has a sharp pain down the left side of her face. Though all the
pain has not disappeared, she feels it is possible that she may
recover with the doctor's help.

It is a warm spring day, and she looks at the smooth blue
sky and listens to the raucous cries of the city birds. It occurs
to her, as she passes a flower vendor in the street, that she
could take a bunch of daffodils to the doctor—now the professor, to congratulate him on his professorship, but she is not
certain how he would interpret such a gesture and decides
against it.

Once again she wonders if he will take her back into
treatment if she asks him. She knows she has a rebellious side

to her nature, that she has fought with him and attempted to thwart his attempts to convince her. But this time she is the one who desires the treatment and not her father. She is going to see him because she thinks he might be of help. She would like to give him another chance to cure her completely. She feels that now, since her visit to the Z.'s, since their confrontation, she will be able to talk with him about other things. Perhaps she will even tell him the truth: that she had stolen from his book, that her dreams were made up for him.

She will definitely tell him about the neuralgia, and she wants to congratulate him on his professorship, which she has read about in the newspaper. She knows how happy he must be about that, and she is happy for him. She has to admit he has acquired added prestige in her eyes as well as society's. Her father has told her how it will change the doctor's life, make it easier now for him to find well-paying patients, to spread his novel ideas. Perhaps it will put him in a good mood with her and enable him to see things differently.

She knows, too, also from her father, that the doctor has finally visited Rome since she last saw him, a city he has always said he longed to reach though she does not quite understand why he never managed to before. Above all, she is eager to let him know what she has accomplished since she left him, fifteen months before. She feels she has used her three months of treatment, despite all her difficulties with him, to good effect.

Despite his grave face and cool reception at the door to his consulting rooms, she smiles warmly at him and walks across the familiar Persian rugs. She has dressed up for this occasion and tied a bright blue ribbon around her neck. She has put on her best blue dress.

Tall glass vases of spring flowers perfume the room sweetly today: long stems of lilac and jasmine spilling over. Perhaps the professor's wife has arranged them, or perhaps some well-wisher has sent them to congratulate him. Through the open window a slight breeze lifts the curtain. She lies down without protest on the silky rug that covers his couch and runs her fingers over the smooth weave.

"It feels so strange to be back here," she says, thinking the room seems larger though even more filled with mysterious objects. Are there new acquisitions among the little statues?

"And how have you been feeling since I last saw you?" he asks her politely enough when he has taken up his habitual pew, giving her the freedom to imagine him as she wishes.

She says, "I am feeling much better. For a while I felt all in a muddle when I first left here, but now I am better, though I have a sharp pain down the left side of my face," and she touches her cheek where it aches.

He immediately interprets this ache in her cheek as a reminder of the slap she gave Herr Z. on *his* cheek at the lake when he had made his proposal. Certainly, he has not forgotten her story. She wonders if it is he who would like to slap *her* for breaking off the therapy, for treating him like a servant, a maid, as he had said, but she keeps that to herself. She does not want to quarrel with him today. She feels grateful to him and she would like him to take her back. So instead she tells him she has been to see the Z.'s, who have recently moved to Vienna.

"Ah! And what prompted your visit?" he asks with some interest.

"It was on a very sad occasion," she says, and the tears come to her eyes as they do so easily at the thought of those near to her whom she has lost. She thinks of her beloved Aunt Malvine, who has died, as she had feared she would during her absence from Vienna.

"Indeed, and why sad?" he asks.

"The occasion of their daughter's death," she says. "Poor little Clara has died, perhaps you know?" she tells him. "She had always had a weak heart, as you probably know, but it was still such a shock to me. I felt so close to her, had spent so much time with her. I loved her so much. She was almost like my own child."

He says it must have been a shock to her.

She was very sad to hear the news, naturally, as she was so fond of the bright little girl, and could hardly believe she was no more. It was through the little girl that they had come to know the couple, the professor—she is careful to call him that now—may remember. "Somehow her death seemed to be the end of an important part of my life. In some way little Clara was my link with her mother and father. When Mother suggested it would be polite to pay a visit to offer our condolences, after only a moment's hesitation, I decided I would indeed go."

"I see," he says.

She had dressed herself up carefully, brushed her hair until it glowed, donned a smart black dress that emphasized her small waist, she admits, put on her best black hat with a little veil and gloves, and gone to see them with her mother at her side. She takes a certain pleasure in telling all of this to him so truthfully.

"And how were they?" he asks, so that she wonders if he has seen them recently himself. "And did you still feel so angry with them?" he asks.

"At first," she says, "I felt nothing but sympathy for both of them. How could I not? I knew they had loved their little girl so much, and they seemed quite bowed down and overcome with grief," she tells him. They huddled together in their silent and well-polished entrance hall, both in deep mourning.

"They looked smaller to me and older. They seemed suddenly a little elderly, harmless couple, bowed down literally with grief."

Frau Z. was wearing a thin black veil, but she could still see that her face was all swollen with weeping. Her lovely, fresh white skin was reddened, and her full lips looked chapped.

"Poor woman! How she must have suffered. What could be more awful than the death of a child and such a sweet, lively one?" she asks him.

"Indeed," he says with feeling.

Many years later she will hear that he, too, has suffered a similar loss. His Sophie, his Sunday child, the most beautiful of his three girls, will die young of the Spanish influenza after the First World War, as will her little Heinele, his favorite grandchild, dying of tuberculosis, only three years after his mother.

"And how did they greet you?" he asks now.

"Frau Z. asked us to come into the parlor and embraced both of us warmly and thanked us for coming," she says.

"And Herr Z.?" the doctor asks.

"Herr Z. shook my hand a little stiffly and bowed over Mother's. Pippina invited me to sit beside her on the red velvet sofa, took my hand, and wept. She could hardly speak she was sobbing so hard. Eventually, she asked us to forgive her— she was overcome, and said it was so good of us both to come and visit. She thanked me in particular for all my help with her little girl in her frequent illnesses. 'She was so fond of you. You were like another mother to her,' she told me and stroked my hand and continued to weep. Herr Z. just sat in silence in the winged leather armchair across the room, his head bowed. He seemed quite defeated," she tells the professor.

A servant brought in the tea tray with the silver samovar and offered them tea and iced pastries from Demel's, which she, who felt suddenly hungry, was the only one to eat. She remembered the first time she had met the Z.'s, that sun-filled moment on the terrace of the hotel in Meran, and how the child had slipped from her wicker chair and come running over to their table spontaneously in her sundress and stood there staring at her. She recalled how she had fed her some of her chocolate cake, so that the little girl had a small mustache of chocolate on her upper lip. She had seemed so lively and well. How could she be gone forever?

"There was the heavy scent of arum lilies in the air, which made my head spin. I still feel giddy sometimes," she tells the professor, and is afraid of fainting. There were huge vases of

flowers everywhere which people must have sent—rather like
the flowers in the professor's room today. "Yet, without the
lively children, the room seemed empty and silent, all the
windows firmly shut on the noises from the street," she says,
listening to the quiet in the professor's room where she has
not been for such a long time.

The little boy had apparently been sent to his grandparents
for a while. His presence only reminded the parents of the
missing child, and they found it quite unbearable, Frau Z. said.

For a while they all talked in subdued voices about the
little girl and how sweet and good she had been. "Such a precious child," Herr Z. said, almost the first words he had managed all afternoon, and as he said them he lifted his gaze and
looked her in the face, and she looked directly back at him
without shame.

"It was then that I found myself speaking, the words just
coming to me despite myself, sitting there beside Pippina in
the shadowy drawing room with the curtains drawn and all
the mirrors veiled, the gas fire burning, the parquet floor
creaking with the footsteps of the heavy servant who was
retreating to the kitchen, and with Mother sitting opposite
me in her black hat and feather, quite unaware of what I was
about to say, smiling approvingly for once and sipping her
tea," she tells him.

"And what did you say?" he asks with what appears genu-
ine interest, and she hears him shifting around in his chair.

"I said that I hoped that now they would acknowledge the
truth, that it was very important to me that my parents know
I was not making this up."

"And how did they respond?" he asks in a severe voice, which surprises her.

They said nothing at first—there was a complete and shocked silence in the room, apart from the ticking of the gold clock on the mantelpiece and the chink of the china cups, which everyone put down at once. Then her mother mumbled something about this not being the moment perhaps to discuss all of this, that they should leave these poor people, who were sufficiently distressed as it was—people who had had enough unhappiness in their lives without her adding to it.

"And so you left?" he asks, and she has the impression he thinks that is what she should have done.

She shakes her head and waves her arm, smooths back her hair, and says firmly, "No, we did not. I remained sitting on the sofa, holding on to the velvet skirt to keep from rising to my feet, though Mother had risen and was hovering nervously over me, her hand on my shoulder. I was determined to say something. After all it was here, in this room, that I learned from you, dear professor, to speak my mind frankly," she tells him with some satisfaction, though she receives no response to this. Perhaps this was not what he had meant?

"It is here that I learned the importance of speaking what comes to mind, and how that can change things," she goes on, nevertheless.

She told the couple that surely now they would feel obliged to acknowledge what had happened.

"And did they?" he asks.

"No, they just sat there with their heads bowed and their

gaze on the carpet, tears on their cheeks." Her mother remained at her side with her hand warningly gripping her
shoulder, saying, "You must understand how this mother and
father feel, surely. Have you no pity?"

"I did feel sorry for them," she admits, "but at the same
time I felt that they should feel pity for me and admit how
they had both betrayed me and used me for their own ends.
They both just went on weeping, until eventually Herr Z.
lifted his head and looked at me and Mother. He said in a low
voice that such things indeed happened all too often in the
best of families, and he had never intended to cause me distress: on the contrary. He looked at his wife and said firmly
that neither of them had. He turned back to me and said that
they had suffered more than anyone could have wished by
losing what was most precious to them."

"And you left then?" he asks in a low voice.

"Then Pippina stumbled to her feet, with a certain dig-
nity, I will admit. She lifted her veil, kissed both of us, and
asked us please to continue to come and see them, and that
she did hope we could all remain friends. And she took my
hand and added, 'If there is anything I can ever do to thank
you for all you did for our Clara, I assure you I will. You can
count on my support, if you should ever need it.'"

And indeed, though she had not believed what Pippina
said at that moment, she will need her support, when both her
parents are dead, her mother at fifty of colon cancer, and her
father, soon afterward. His money will be lost soon after the
First World War with the defeat of the Austro-Hungarian
Empire and with the Depression.

During the years between the wars, when bridge has become all the rage, she and Pippina will make a living by teaching the game to the society ladies of Vienna. Together they will be "bridge mistresses." They will rent a "Bridgestube" and sit opposite each other for long, quiet afternoons among rich ladies in flowered hats and kid gloves in rooms filled with smoke and polished silver and flowers, while the servants bring in tea and the cakes from Demel's. They will play endless games in the big rooms with only the sound of the buzzing of a fly, the ticking of the clock, the bidding, and the slap of cards on the table. She will remember instinctively each card that has been played. She will know how to chest her cards, how to send out subtle, almost invisible signs to her oldest and dearest friend: a slight widening of the eyes in disagreement, a sliver of a smile of consent, a lowered glance of warning, a frown of puzzlement. Without any men around them they are able to understand each other completely, using only the coded language of cards.

Later, when the Nazis are hunting for her because of Otto's Marxist affiliations, Pippina will hide her in spite of great personal danger, events she could not have foreseen that day in their parlor, as she stood so defiantly before them in her black dress.

But back then, in their shadowy, sad parlor, she tells the professor, she turned away from Pippina, saying only, "I am so very sad about poor little Clara. I will never forget her or either of you."

She will remember them also when she later stands in endless queues, repeatedly told she lacks a document, or must come up with more money, if she is to be allowed to leave the country. She will go first to Paris, invited by Léon Blum, and then be driven from Paris to the South of France. She will go on to Casablanca, where she contracts cholera and lies helplessly in a hospital bed as her visa expires. Finally, thanks to her son's connections, she is able to escape to Chicago, just as the doctor himself will one day go to England, leaving this city he both hates and loves.

"And you told your father about this meeting, I suppose?" the professor asks.

"Indeed I did, the moment we got home. I found Father in his study and stood before his big, pompous desk and reported our conversation. At first he looked appalled and asked me what had come over me. He said I had taken advantage of these poor people in a moment of distress, that I was a difficult child, who had caused him much grief. When I protested, and reported Pippina's words, he finally said he hoped, indeed, that now we could all be on friendly terms once again and that he would certainly not bring up the matter again. He was glad to hear that I had not been lying to him," she tells him, thinking that the only person she has lied to is himself, and that it was in her father's study that she had found his book on dreams, which she had used to inspire her.

She tells the professor she saw Herr Z. once more, by such a curious chance, that if it were not true, would seem fabricated, something out of a story. She was with her maid on a busy street, doing an errand for her mother. She had just come out of a ribbon shop, when, to her surprise, she caught sight of him. He looked up and saw her as he was crossing the street and turned to stare at her. He was so distracted that he seemed blinded and stood there motionless in the sunlight for a moment too long, and he had been knocked over by a cart. She says she remained on the pavement, watching, unable to move, and felt all the blood drain from her head. She was so upset she almost fainted, as she had once after a quarrel with her father, though she realized Herr Z. had not been seriously harmed. She watched as he picked himself up, recovered his hat, brushed himself off, and went on his way.

"So you feel you have had your revenge on him and perhaps on me, too?" the professor asks.

"I have not come back here for revenge, but on the contrary to thank you and tell you what I have managed to accomplish since I left. I was even hoping that now you might take me back," she says.

"That would no longer be possible," he says, petulantly. He is not a forgiving man, she thinks. Does he hold grudges, just discard people after using them, or is he simply impulsive and a bit adolescent, himself, as she was?

"I have learned a lot from you, and though I still don't agree with everything you suggested, it has been very useful to me," she says, as politely as possible, blinking back her tears.

But the professor remains silent. She will have to face the future without him, and perhaps it is better like this. However diminished she is, she is now free, her own, last authority. She will have to decide what is right for herself. She will have to reclaim some of her old wildness, her belief in her own capacity to judge for herself. And she will. *She will!*

Still, there are so many things she does not understand about their interaction. "Why did you always take Herr Z.'s side? Is he a friend or perhaps even a patient of yours? Was Pippina your patient?" she inquires, as she sits up and turns toward him, but can see from his closed and angry face that the man has no intention of divulging *his* secrets.

Indeed, she suspects now—correctly, as it turns out—that she will never see him again.

1901–1939

XXIV

FAME

THE PROFESSOR DOES NOT PUBLISH his manuscript immediately. He calls the first draft "Dreams and Hysteria: A Fragment of an Analysis." It lies in his desk until he has more news of his former patient. She and her husband have had a son. She will have moved on, and his time with her will no longer have the same importance it did initially. This son will replace the other men in her life. He feels he can now, in good conscience, take the manuscript out of the drawer and send it on to his publisher.

His collection of beautiful objects, which will grow over the years, will one day be packed up and saved from the Nazis. His sister-in-law, Minna, his wife, Martha, and the children, his own doctor, that man's wife, his maids, and his dog, too, will escape with him to England.

How could he envisage that the very rooms in which he had heard so much about the beginnings of the lives of his patients will serve as a Nazi transit station, where Jews will be penned before being sent off to their deaths, his sisters, including his favorite, Rosa, among them. All will die except for Anna, the oldest, who, as a young girl, was not allowed to practice the piano, because it bothered her brilliant brother. Rosa will one day tell the commandant in the concentration camp that she is Sigmund Freud's sister, and he will tell her that, in that case, there must have been some mistake, and that she must take the next train out, only first she needs to have a shower.

As for the doctor's text, it is not until three years after their final visit that he publishes his account. It will serve as a model for students of the analytic process, truncated though it may be. He imagines that his followers will read and discuss it avidly. How much ink will spill because of it! This "fragment of an analysis," as he calls it, these broken pieces of her life and of his own, will finally bring him the fame he covets.

Over the years, as he grows more and more famous and the pain from the cancer eating away at his jaw increases, the girl, whom, incidentally, he has made infamous, will come back to him at times when he sits alone in the silence of his study. She will stand before him as she did that first afternoon, at seventeen, in her white dress with its green sash, trembling slightly, moving her hands in the air, her bracelets jingling, her large lucent eyes filled with anger and hope.

DECEMBER 1945

———

XXV

LUCK

Last night, lying alone in her narrow bed in Brooklyn, she dreamed she was a spaniel puppy with long blond ears and no body. Somehow she was able to move around on those ears alone. She still wears her hair long, though it is quite white now. It was a dream she would like to have taken to the professor. Its meaning is clear to her: her body, so full of pain, has dropped away.

Memories are part of her suffering body, like the heart that pumps the blood through her veins. Even during her long flight from danger, her adolescent days of shame and rage came back to her, and she would stare up at the stars in the South of France and think back to something dark and poisonous that crawled its way into her mind: those moments of her late adolescence when she had been accused of making up stories about her father's friend.

The morning light filters through the thin yellow curtains. Why would anyone put up such useless things? She listens to the sounds from the street and remembers the lonely sounds of the trains she could hear during the sleepless nights in Vienna. Sleep eludes her here, too. She wakes before dawn. Perhaps she should have moved the flowers. A neighbor has thoughtfully brought a small bouquet of flowers and placed it on her dresser: bright pink carnations, which she has never liked, because the petals look as if they have been stained artificially with pink ink and which are said to take up the oxygen in the night. Perhaps she is too old to sleep much. Yet, oddly, she does not feel old at sixty-three, despite the pain in her body and her lack of energy. Her mind is as active as ever, perhaps more so, with all the memories, all the life contained within her. Is all of this to be lost? Will no one share it? Yet she felt older at seventeen, hovering at the top of the stairs in a rage, making her father wait for her. Now she waits for her boy to come in the door for Christmas.

Is it possible, now that she is safe, that all of this could come to an end? Not now, she thinks, not like this. Am I going to die alone? She is certain the doctor she saw yesterday will contact her son. Surely he will come?

She celebrated her birthday almost two months ago at a splendid dinner at the Plaza, followed by a carriage ride in the park, all the brilliant leaves, impossible splashes of red and gold that she has never seen anywhere else amazing her. With her were her son and her new American daughter-in-law with their new daughter in her frilly pink dress and lace panties. As she held the plump little rosy-cheeked girl squirming in her arms, she had thought of her own baby boy.

How his birth had surprised her! Perhaps all of life has surprised her, not always in welcome ways. Her son had arrived two months before he was expected, and so painfully. How little her mother had conveyed of the difficulties she would have to face. She remembers her mother saying, "You will forget the pain the moment they put the baby in your arms." But she had not forgotten! She had not! She had never wanted to do it again.

She remembers having told the professor she would never marry, never bear a child, that all men were traitors. And she was not wrong: even he, sitting behind her, was only waiting for her to tell him what he wanted to hear, and when she demurred, like a child in a tantrum, he would turn his face to the wall. Only her son has not betrayed her, not until now. Yet the desire to hold something so small and fragile in her own arms, that rush of tenderness, that need to protect, to shelter, to console—must always have been there, somewhere within her body, like a seed or a stone, planted deep within her flesh, immutable, even as, at eighteen, she sat in the museum in Dresden and stared at Raphael's Madonna and Child.

She had begun to feel the labor pains before daybreak on a Sunday morning on the first of April. She had awakened her husband, who did not like his sleep disturbed, hesitantly, not quite sure if this were true or if it were simply an urge to relieve herself. "I think the baby is coming," she had said shyly. He had groaned unsympathetically, unconvinced. "You had better call the doctor," she urged a few moments later, unaware of how long the process would last.

And it had seemed to last endlessly, people coming and going confusingly around her, voices hushing her screams, telling her to bear down. She was determined the child would be born before midnight. She so desired a Sunday child, a lucky child, the kind she had never been. She fought mightily to push this heart and flesh forth, feeling it tear her flesh asunder. How joyously she had heard his cry, how fiercely she had held the baby boy in her arms, before the chimes of midnight. Clinging on to this part of her, this heart grown from her own, she had thought then that she would always have him, no matter what happened, that he would be there to listen to her heart beat its last, her life ebbing. Has her luck run out?

Yet her boy has been so lucky and brought her luck. He has led a charmed life, leaving Czechoslovakia the day before the Nazis overran it, finding a passage on that Dutch boat and arriving in this country. He has always been surrounded by women who adore him. He has been successful already, as chorus master of the San Francisco Opera, discovering great, new voices, though she could not know that among them were to be Beverly Sills, Leontyne Price, Luciano Pavarotti.

He has managed to rescue her and bring her here.

She still remembers lying on the long veranda in that wretched Casablanca hospital, open to the elements, discarded there like refuse, on a lumpy pallet, with the flies, the heat, the putrid smells of death, the desperate moans and cries all around her through the long nights. It had seemed to her that the brilliant world of her youth, the world of art and song—beauty in all its varied forms—had come to an end, swept away by such cruelty and bestiality.

Obliged to flee first from Vienna and then from France, she had escaped to Casablanca only to contract cholera there, her body burning up with fever, her limbs shaking, liquid leaking from all her orifices. She told the young Arab nurse who leaned over her in his white robe that she wanted to be left in peace to die. Such a fine-looking man—despite her agony she noticed that—he was trying to sponge her brow with a cool cloth, to bring down the fever, telling her in French that she must not die, not now. She remembers him announcing in his hopeful, grating voice that there was a letter for her. She shook her head, waving him away, unable to believe that anyone could even know where she was, let alone send her a letter. Yet her heart had tilted with hope as he pressed it into her hands, and she recognized the familiar writing, so much like her own. Through a mist of fever and pain, her hands shaking, convinced she must be inventing the blurred words before her eyes, she managed to read the few lines from her son, telling her that he had contacted the consulate through influential people he knew, and that he would be sending the money for her ticket to America. She must get well enough to travel. He had found a way to bring her to him, her Sunday boy.

She has lived for him and through him for so many years. She remembers his first years in Vienna: the carriage rides through the Prater, his little, white-gloved hands neatly on his lap; their summers in Alter Aussee, the bicycling, swimming, and the hikes they did with her friend Hannah, who had rented a house for them and for Hannah's child, who is now her doctor in New York; her boy's sight reading, at thirteen, *Die Walküre* on the piano, amazing his teacher; his work with Max Reinhardt and Toscanini in Salzburg; and finally, at the last moment, the invitation to come to Chicago to coach a singer there.

From the bed where she lies now, she looks around the small, neat room he has found for her, with its bare walls and floor, the deal table with the flowers, a lace doily beneath the glass vase, and the photo of him as a little boy, holding her hand. In it he turns his narrow face up to her, squinting in the sunlight, and not looking into the camera, as his father was telling him to do. They are standing in the gravel driveway beside their shiny gun-metal-gray car. How proud her husband was of that car! One of the very first private ones in Vienna, he usually kept it at her father's factory, but this Sunday he had brought it to Dobling, to take the family for a drive in the lovely, leafy suburb. She can still see the fence with the pink, climbing roses behind her and her little son.

What joy she had felt on leaving her parents' somber house on Lichtensteinstrasse, where she had been so unhappy, moving on, at last, as a young married woman with her tall, handsome husband and small, lively, auburn-haired boy. Once again she was entering those big, bright rooms, surrounded by packing cases, listening to the birdsong and watching the leaves of the lindens fluttering outside the window. Her boy had stood beside her, smiling like a little cherub in a beam of light. She had picked him up and swung him around in the air, and she had thought that the world, for the moment, was good.

She does not remember now how old he was when they moved to Dobling, such a fashionable district, where Beethoven was born. He could have been no more than three, though he always said afterward that he remembered that move, remembered the surprise of coming into those big light rooms, though surely he was too young and could not possibly have remembered such a thing. She sees it now clearly: the three floors in the quiet villa on a tree-lined street, the big airy rooms filled with sunlight; the new, modern furniture, with its severe, simple lines and light wood; the marquetry of her old desk, where she kept her diary—she must still have it somewhere, with its inscription from the professor's book on dreams.

What she now sees so vividly in her mind, the image coming to her repeatedly in the silence and loneliness of the early hour, are the little ancient statues on the professor's desk. She sees him picking them up and putting them down, and she sees her father in the carriage that day he dragged her there, leaning forward out of the shadows, as they went down the hill. She hears him calling the professor a "miracle worker." She had indeed considered him a magician, a clever one, but hardly a real doctor, surrounded by his magic objects, a doctor whom her family might well not have allowed through their front door but rather, the tradesmen's entrance. He had listened and observed and believed what she had said, encouraging her as no one else did at the time, and had enabled her, ultimately, to confront the Z.'s in ways he might not have intended—the confrontation certainly not part of her father's devious plan.

Still her father had been generous enough with her and her husband, she reflects—or was he just happy to pay the price to have his recalcitrant daughter out of the house?—to take his son-in-law into his business, despite his disapproval. She remembers her father even hiring an entire orchestra and a concert hall and rounding up friends and family so that her husband could have the pleasure of hearing his minor music played in public to generous applause.

Certainly her brother was suspicious of her husband from the start. "A very charming man," she remembers Otto saying in a way that made the words sound like an insult. She remembers all the insults in their house.

Yet soon after her mother's death, her father had become ill. He did not live long after her mother died of the same illness she suffers from today. She was obliged anew to become her father's nurse, as she had been as a child. And now who will watch over the end of *her* days? Her son has promised to come in time for Christmas, but will she still be here?

For a moment she thinks she has heard the telephone ring and starts to rise from her bed, hastily picking up her pink flannel gown, pulling it about her shoulders, shuffling on her slippers, before realizing it is just the ringing in her ears and collapsing back down onto her bed.

Her son, busy with his successful career and his own family on the West Coast, has rarely had time to visit. He has been too busy establishing the career in music her poor husband would so much have liked to have. She sees her boy crouching on the floor under the grand piano, listening attentively to her husband's compositions, which even then she doubted would be remembered. She recalls him teaching their little boy the Hungarian folk dances he had learned as a small child. How she had laughed at him! Opening up his little arms like a window and turning on his toes.

She recalls that moment in the Kalmberg, one sunny afternoon, sitting outside around a table with a prominent friend, a bank director—she can no longer remember his name—someone whom they knew well, all of them drinking coffee. They were all talking and laughing. A military band was playing in the background, when the director was called to the telephone, and the military band stopped playing. Her boy said, visibly shocked, "How could they stop playing in the middle of a bar!" It was then that their friend came back to the table and announced the shooting of the crown prince in Sarajevo, and she realized the gravity of the event, but what had struck her son was the interruption of a military band in midbar.

Yet the music lessons continued through the war years despite her husband's absence, the lack of heat and light, using kerosene lamps.

After the war, when Austria became a republic, she made sure her brother, a famous Socialist politician, introduced her boy to the important people in the government, even the president, who took him to his heart and allowed him to sit in the imperial box at the opera, though the box was no longer imperial but only social-democratic. Her husband, who was a snob at heart, a man who was impressed by tradition and the aristocracy, someone who loved fine clothes and fine food, did not get on with Otto from the start, disapproving of his Socialist ideals.

She has a sudden memory of him standing in the shadows of the hallway of the apartment, having just come back from a business trip, or what he had called a business trip—he was always off somewhere, happy to escape the home, with his special suitcase in hand, a suitcase made to hold his record player, a big old heavy thing, with a horn, carrying his music around with him, listening to it wherever he traveled.

How ironic that he would come back from the war wounded and deaf in his left ear, a man irreparably damaged in body and spirit. They would have to shout at him to get him to hear anything, and when they did, he would be offended. "You don't have to scream at me like that!" he would say, looking hurt. "I'm not completely deaf!" He was now an altered man, given to sudden, inexplicable rages, storming around the house, finding fault with the maids, with her, reminding her of no one so much as her own mother, of all people. Unable to work, to play his music, or even to converse with his friends, he was miserable and bent on making all those around him equally so. It was only thanks to her father that they had managed to continue living comfortably, at least for a while, despite her husband's incapacity to work.

Like so many in her family, he was to die young, and, ironically, on Christmas day. Will her fate be the same? How desperately she had tried to find a doctor to help while her husband lay through the night in such pain, but by the time someone came it was too late. Then she had nothing left except for her boy.

All her dreams, her real dreams, were for this sensitive, high-strung, and gifted boy, her lucky Sunday child. She would lie under the duvet at night beside her husband and dream of his future. And she had not only dreamed! She did not rely on luck alone. She had made sure he would acquire the serious musical education she had never been given, as well as complete his rigorous studies at the gymnasium, which she had not been allowed to attend. She stood waiting for him at the bus stop when he came home from school in the afternoon, to make sure he would not slip out to play with the girls. She made sure he finished all his homework and would be *primus* in his class.

She would call him into her room as soon as she had his marks in hand, and if any of them were less than perfect, she would scold. She can see him in her bedroom, standing there awkwardly looking around at the sea-green counterpane, the sea-green curtains, the dressing table with its ruffle around the edge. He would draw himself up, scowling at her reproaches and saying, "I am doing my best, Mother."

She would reply, "You have to do *better* than your best."

And he did work so hard! So hard!

He slept little and was endlessly active. Later, he became opinionated, holding forth as though he knew all on various subjects, but at the same time he was a devious child, finding some way to slip out the door and escape her surveillance. He would come up with some trumped-up excuse, which she could see was false but was unable to disprove. Yet over the years he was always so loving, so charming, so endearing, elegant like his father, with his father's good bone structure, the long narrow feet, the aristocratic profile, the sensuous lips, the deep blue eyes.

Though they have often fought, sometimes bitterly—they are far too similar and too headstrong, not to fight—she admires his determination, his perfectionism, and above all his musical ability.

And how she had plotted and planned his splendid future, making him speak nothing but French for a while—no German, and then English, and on to Italian, over all his protests. Yet all his languages have been useful to him, they have! She remembers his departure for Italy when the Germans would not renew his work permit, going back, coincidentally, to Meran, where she and the Z.'s had summered. Not to mention his facility with English, which she had taught him, and which allowed him to coach the singer in Chicago.

She had sent him to the best music teachers, beginning with the old one, who would wait at the door of his tiny studio at the top of his house, with his beard and his black cap on his head, to teach him harmony.

Music was a major part of their lives. They would walk for miles to the opera if necessary when the trolley was not running, after the war. She remembers her boy—he must have been six years old—sitting solemnly in his little black suit at Mahler's funeral.

Her doctor, one of her boy's oldest friends, is also a music lover. He, too, escaped to America at the last minute. He will give him the news about her illness. She has not wanted to complain about her deteriorating health. After all, her son is now the chorus master of the opera in San Francisco, able both to conduct and to spot new talent, the things her husband would have longed to do.

And how lucky she was to have found Pippina when her father's money was running out. She remembers standing in a breadline during the Depression, when she noticed a woman who still had something proud about the carriage of her head, the stretch of the neck, the blond hair, threaded with gray but neatly plaited and twisted up on the top of her head, the mysterious smile. In her worn black dress, with a wicker basket on her arm, Pippina was unrecognizable at first. Gone were the ringlets, gone was the crescent-shaped diamond brooch in her hair, the bright stones on her busy, small fingers. Gone even the extravagant hats with their feathers and bows. It was Pippina who had recognized her.

"I would know that lovely face anywhere," she had said, clasping her tightly, putting her hand to her hair to push it back from her brow. They had repaired joyfully to a coffeehouse, a dark place in the basement of a building nearby, but life seemed suddenly brighter, lit up by Pippina's presence. There, over the small wooden table in the smoke-filled air, they had hatched their scheme. Pippina had spoken first of their financial difficulties, the move to a smaller shop, the refusal by the factories to provide the necessary supplies on credit, the orders trickling in and then drying up completely, the bankruptcy, and the sale of the shop with all its contents—all those lovely hats—for a song! She and her husband were nearly destitute.

She, too, had sighed and said times were so hard for all of them. Her father's factories had been sold for very little, and her husband was unable to work at all.

Pippina reached across the table and took her hands and turned them over and looked at how red they had become, as she said, "I remember how good you were at bridge. Do you remember how we played endless games on the terrace in that beautiful hotel?"

It was then that she had the idea for the "Bridgestube."

"But who would come to learn bridge now? Who has the money?" Pippina had asked.

"There are always those who are able to take advantage of the despair of others, as I have learned so well!" she had said.

It was she who had rented the room where they taught together in the afternoons, and she who hired the maids to bring in the tea and cakes. They had become a successful team, teaching rich ladies without much skill. She had discovered her talents as an organizer, a diplomat, talents she had only used up until then with her son.

Now Pippina has perished like so many.

Now, so near her own death, she rarely listens to music, except to the radio in the afternoon in the tiny, spotlessly clean kitchen, while she knits sweaters for her little granddaughter. She has little energy or appetite today. How strange that she should have ended up in this unknown part of the world, eating this flavorless food, alone. She misses the fresh, dark bread of Vienna.

She remembers those rare, calm, sunny mornings in the mountains, picnicking with her boy, along with her dear friend Hannah, and Hannah's boy: the sound of rushing water, the clear white mountain light filtering through the leaves, the thick pieces of dark bread and butter. Here the bread tastes rather like cardboard.

On bright days she sits in the leafy places in Prospect Park. She watches the trees, the sky, and the birds. Yesterday, she saw a bright, cheeky cardinal on a branch who fluttered there for a while by her side like life, staring at her with his black face and pointed red cap and seeming quite unafraid. Rather pompously, he gave her a little sermon before flying away with a bright flash of wings.

She tries not to think or to fantasize, but the thoughts of her past come unbidden. She remembers her boy as a defenseless baby, his fears, his insecurities, and the small cruelties which enabled him to become the man he is today. There are a few friends of the family nearby whom he has been able to help, and who call on her, bringing fruit or flowers and occasionally a bottle of white sparkling wine. It is thanks to her son that they have managed to get here.

Since the operation she has taken little nourishment. She wishes the doctors had left her alone; the pain is back in her abdomen anyway, and she knows the cancer is growing. At least she has left the hospital. She prefers to be in her own place, even alone. She moves quietly within the four walls of her room, finding her way by instinct, as though she were blind. She hears a loud buzzing in her ears. She is so accustomed to this continuous buzzing that she hardly notices it now, though the doctor—how many doctors she has seen in her life!—this one, surely the most disagreeable of men, whom she saw once or perhaps twice in Vienna, after the first war, said it might be caused by her constant listening for the return of her son, who would come home so late at night as an adolescent. She knew he was out with one pretty girl after another and worried so about him. Now, once again, she listens for the telephone to ring.

From the start, even in primary school, he was a great favorite with the girls. She remembers little Lotte, with her blond plaits, the first one, whom he fell asleep next to in kindergarten. A handsome boy, like her father, with his bright auburn locks that she could not bring herself to cut until he was almost three.

"Tell me the truth," she had said to the doctor, looking into his eyes. "I've known you too long for you to deceive me." After a moment of silence he had looked down at his desk and then said to her, "If there is anything you want to do, do it now." She understood that not much time remained.

Perhaps her son will simply find a place on an airplane and come directly to her without bothering to telephone. Perhaps he will ring her doorbell and she will find him there with a bunch of flowers in his hands.

Is it possible to envisage one's own death, she wonders, looking out the window? It has begun to snow, the snow-flakes large and wet, melting before they reach the ground, the sky a strange gray. Or does one just keep hoping up until the end, until the last moment? How can the world go on without her there to record what is happening? How can she imagine that she might never get to tell her story, even to her son, that all that will be left of her eventful life will be the record the professor made of a brief period in her youth?

She has read that record. Some of it had amused her, particularly the importance given to the two dreams she had made up for him. But how will her boy continue without her? She feels he, too, is partly her invention, held aloft by her will, her hopes and dreams.

She thinks of her diary of imaginary events—is it still hidden away in the bottom drawer of her dresser, with its faded blue cover, an object light and small enough to bring with her on her voyage, with the funny drawings of her mother's green hat and the golden *SS* snakes intertwined? What seems so surprising to her was her adolescent interest in what she called rather grandly matters of the mind, her desire to find the answers to all the unanswerable questions, her intellectual strivings, her search for truth, as though such a thing could be found. What was she thinking? How impractical and misguided she had been, with no one to show her the way. No wonder she had clung to women like the charming, fickle Pippina, whose openness had seemed so fascinating in comparison to her own mother's constricted view of the world, someone who had betrayed her and yet whom she had turned to for support.

And what about the professor? What will history say about him?

She remembers his quiet room, his little statues, and the silky carpet that covered the couch where she lay. She remembers wondering what he wanted her to tell him. She certainly tried to oblige. She has never quite understood why he was so cross with her, why he felt she was dismissing him like an unruly servant, when she told him she was leaving. Why had he not understood that she was trying to get him to pay attention to her, indeed, to ask her to stay? She realizes now that he, too, was at the beginning of his career and still finding his way. He has used her words to describe their work together. She is glad if she has provided him with some of the material that has helped him to change the way the world sees itself.

She wonders if he was aware of the role of luck in his own life.

He seemed to think his words could change things, could make the lame walk, the deaf hear, and the blind see. Perhaps they have.

She has become famous, too, she thinks, smiling at the irony of it all. Her imaginings have been examined and interpreted again and again. How many people have already taken up her story and filled in the blank spaces, attempting to explicate what happened according to their own imaginative desires? At least her sufferings have served a purpose, and a good one, at that. The professor's version of their interaction is so different from what she remembers, but does it matter in the end? Who will have the last word? Will anyone guess that the dreams she told him were invented? Perhaps it does not matter. Perhaps it makes no difference whether the world knows her version of what happened. Would the stars change? Would they cease to glitter so brightly? Would even her own life, what may be left of it, be any different?

Does it matter that her own story may never be told, even to her boy? Who could tell it?

ACKNOWLEDGMENTS

THOUGH THIS BOOK IS A novel and its characters fictive I remain indebted to the many writers, editors, and interviews which helped me to imagine Ida Bauer, Sigmund Freud, and Vienna at the turn of the century: Harry Abrams, Kurt Herbert Adler, Lisa Appignanesi, Didier Anzieu, Janine Burke, Charles Bernheimer, T. Bonyhady, C. Brandstatter, Peter Buckley, Helene Cixous, Hannah Decker, Felix Deutsch, Erik Erikson, John Forrester, Simon Goldhill, Johann von Goethe, Georges Didi-Huberman, Hugo von Hofmannsthal, Alisa Hartz, Asti Hustvedt, Ernest Jones, Eric Kandel, Claire Kahane, Jacques Lacan, Patrick Mahoney, Janet Malcolm, Stephen Marcus, Jeffrey Masson, Guy de Maupassant, Howard Markel, J. Piaget, Joseph Roth, D. M. Thomas, Richard Webster, Edmund de Waal, Stefan Zweig, and particularly Peter Gay as well as Freud's own early letters—especially those to Fliess—Freud and Breuer's *Studies on Hysteria* and Freud's *The Interpretation of Dreams, Fragment of an Analysis of a Case of Hysteria*, and *A Child Is Being Beaten*.

The two dreams quoted in the novel are from *Fragment of an Analysis of a Case of Hysteria* (translated by William Tucker).

I am very grateful to the American Academy in Rome for two summer stays which enabled me to research Freud in Rome.

I would like to thank Maxine Antel for reading my text in an early stage and particularly my eldest daughter, Sasha Troyan, for her generous and inestimable help with this manuscript.

And again, great thanks to my faithful agent of many years and many books, Robin Straus; to my publisher and editor at Penguin, Kathryn Court, for her vision and good judgment, and to Tara Singh.

DREAMING FOR FREUD

Sheila Kohler

An Introduction to
Dreaming for Freud

*"Now he will pin her down with his pen like a
butterfly on the page for posterity" (p. 184).*

In October 1900, a beautiful seventeen-year-old girl begins therapy
with Dr. Sigmund Freud. Formerly healthy and robust, she is
now hobbled by unexplained physical ailments. At forty-four, the
ambitious doctor has already achieved some modest recognition for
his studies into the human mind, albeit less than he desires. Their
sessions last only three months, but both Freud and the girl—
whom he calls "Dora" when he publishes his case study—will be
forever changed by their brief time together.

At first, the young girl dismisses Freud as another member of
Vienna's well-to-do Jewish bourgeoisie. "How could such a boring,
middle-aged man, with his silly pinstriped pants . . . understand
the strange story she has to tell?" (p. 43). Moreover, other doctors
have subjected her to painful and humiliating treatments and she
isn't eager for more. Freud's interest in her is twofold. His recent
book on dream interpretation was not the success he expected, and
"His critics have accused him of not giving verifiable examples to
back up his theories. Perhaps this patient . . . will provide some"
(pp. 25–26). Freud, with a large family to support and a dwindling
clientele, desperately needs the money her wealthy father will
pay him.

3

For his part, her father seeks more than his daughter's return to health from her sessions with Freud. She has accused a family friend of forcing unwanted attentions upon her and, in turn, accused her father of attempting to trade her favors to this man so that her father can continue his own affair with the man's wife. Her father insists that she is lying and wants Freud to convince her to recant. The girl knows that her father has already told Freud that she is untrustworthy and influenced by unsuitable literature. But Freud reassures her, saying, "I need you to simply tell me freely and frankly what comes to your mind without censoring your thoughts. . . . I would like to hear your side of the story" (p. 33). Unlike her other doctors, Freud seems to want only to listen.

"I am an ordinary girl, except for my recent illness" (p. 42), she obligingly begins. But as her story unspools, it is clear that the girl, in fact, considers herself wild, clever, and perhaps even a budding genius. Yet she does more than talk. She observes her observer. "She wonders whether the doctor has so many art objects in his cluttered consulting rooms because he is afraid of emptiness, of space, of silence" (p. 49). She reads his book on dreams and offers to share her own. And in return, she allows Freud to see himself in ways that are both liberating and deeply unsettling. Years after she abruptly leaves his care, Freud's *Dora: An Analysis of a Case of Hysteria* immortalizes her.

Novelist Sheila Kohler is internationally acclaimed for her spare storytelling style and probing psychological insights. In *Dreaming for Freud*, she builds upon the known facts of Freud's and Dora's lives to brilliantly reimagine the story behind one of psychology's most famous and controversial works.

ABOUT THE AUTHOR

Sheila Kohler was born in Johannesburg, South Africa. She lived in Paris before moving to the United States in 1981 to earn her MFA in writing from Columbia University. She studied psychology in France at the Institut Catholique and worked at the Pitié-Salpêtrière Hospital, where Freud studied with Charcot. Sheila currently teaches at Princeton University. *Dreaming for Freud* is her thirteenth work of fiction. She lives in New York City.

A CONVERSATION WITH SHEILA KOHLER

What inspired you to write about the relationship between Sigmund Freud and Dora, the young woman who was arguably his most famous patient?

I earned a degree in psychology in France and actually worked in the hospital where Freud worked with Charcot for a year. I read the five great case histories by Freud and was fascinated by his brilliance and understanding. They made a lasting impression on me: I even imagined that I was becoming hysterical as Freud believed Dora was, when I felt ill on a plane going out to South Africa. When I arrived I saw a doctor who told me I had contracted the measles from one of my children!

Years later I reread the Dora case and saw it through a rather different lens, and like many was shocked at some of the things the young doctor told this very young and vulnerable girl.

In the novel, you write that Freud "has read a great deal of fiction in many languages and knows how to tell a story . . . so as to pique the interest of the reader and catch him in his net" (p. 184). Is there any chance that Dora: An Analysis of a Case of Hysteria *is as much fiction as fact?*

Certainly it can be read as fiction and makes a fascinating story. It is impossible for us to know how close to the truth this case history is. Did Dora tell Freud the truth? Were Freud's interpretations correct? These were some of the questions I asked myself. Freud is most persuasive and writes so clearly and so well. He received the Goethe prize but never the Nobel for his scientific discoveries.

Would you say that all novelists are—in some sense—students of psychology?

Writers need surely to be acute and perceptive observers of human nature. Reading the great writers one is always struck at their comprehension: How could he/she possibly have known that?

How much of your version of Dora's life is based upon that of the real Dora, Ida Bauer? Do you suspect that Dora's dreams were too similar to those in Freud's The Interpretation of Dreams *to actually be real?*

I have tried in the book not to falsify what has been documented, but as always in historical fiction there is so much we do not know. How do we know that the dreams Dora tells Freud she dreamed had not been made up? Some of Freud's patients definitely made up dreams for him in order to please him, and Dora's dreams with their jewel boxes and train stations do sound, at least to our modern ears, perfectly Freudian!

In your novel, Freud's sessions with Dora lead him to an epiphany about his relationship with his friend and colleague, Wilhelm Fliess. Did Freud ever write anything about this? If not, what first led you to this conclusion?

We have Freud's many interesting letters to Fliess, whom he calls his "other." Some of these letters were initially suppressed but are now accessible in their entirety. It was during the three months that Freud was seeing Dora that Fliess distances himself from Freud, who had come to count on him in so many different ways and particularly as a reader and critic of his work.

What is your opinion of the man who is both hailed as the father of psychoanalysis and vilified as a phallocentric male who was deluded about female sexuality?

I think we tend today to see Freud in extremes: we are blinded by his stature and the attraction or repulsion of his theories. I have tried in this book to see him rather as a human being, albeit a genius, with the failings and insecurities and longings of all human beings, a young doctor at the start of his career with the need to support a large family. I've tried to enter his mind and see him more as a creature of his time and place, Vienna 1900, with its growing anti-Semitism and the dangers of syphilis and other sexually transmitted diseases, but at the same time an enchanting great city with all the excitement of new scientific discoveries, art, and music.

You have written some novels with wholly fictional protagonists and some based upon historical figures, including Charlotte Brontë,

Marguerite Duras, and, now, Sigmund Freud. Which do you find more enjoyable to write?

I enjoy the process of writing whether it is straight fiction or historical fiction. I feel very privileged to be able to do something I love. Of course, it is always difficult, and historical fiction has many pitfalls. As Henry James said, how does one reproduce the speech of another age? Indeed, dialogue is one of the most difficult parts, but the research required for historical fiction is fascinating to me. I am endlessly curious about how things happened and why, both in the present and in the past. The process of writing fiction is for me simply an attempt to answer that question. What happened during those three months that Ida Bauer spent going daily (except Sundays) to see Sigmund Freud, and why did she refuse to go after that? What happened to her after that? What happened in the dark room as Charlotte Brontë sat by her father's bedside and wrote *Jane Eyre*?

You often depict characters who are disempowered and trapped in a relationship with a domineering personality, but in Dreaming for Freud, *Dora and Freud appear to be evenly matched. Did you realize this when you set out, or did it become apparent as you were writing the novel?*

Yes, I think both Freud and Dora struggled valiantly from the start and I was not at all sure who would win or if anyone did. They both had considerable ammunition and in my version of the story they used it.

Do you prefer reading fiction or nonfiction? Who are some contemporary writers that you admire?

I love fiction and I read voraciously. I try to keep up with the new books appearing, and continue to go back to the classics. I am a great admirer of J. M. Coetzee and loved his new novel, *The Childhood of Jesus*. I recently read *The Silent Wife* by A. S. A. Harrison, which I thought very well written and tense, as well as a book by Juan Gabriel Vásquez, *The Sound of Things Falling*, which I admired.

Your novels are always very slender and written in the exquisitely spare prose for which you are so often praised. Could you ever imagine publishing a five-hundred or even a thousand-page novel? How much of what you initially write ends up in the novel's final edit?

No, I cannot imagine writing something that long. I do a lot of revision and often discard a great many unnecessary words! I am aware, however, that the long novel seems to be in vogue.

What are you working on now?

I am working on a novel, which is somewhat longer than usual, about a child who disappears on a beach in Brittany. The tentative title is *To Bear My Soul Away*.

SUGGESTED QUESTIONS
FOR DISCUSSION

1. When Dora arrives at Freud's office, she suffers from uncontrollable fits of coughing, constipation, and mysterious pains. Do you believe they are contrived or caused by her mental and emotional distress?

2. Is Dora's father genuinely concerned for her welfare, or—as she suspects—does he want her to give herself to Herr Z. so that he can continue his affair with Frau Z.?

3. To what do you attribute Freud's passion for artifacts and antiquities?

4. Why does Dora take such care to dress well for her visits to Freud?

5. In telling Freud about her brother, Otto, Dora laments, "In the beginning, I could keep up with my brother, as he shared many of the books he read at the *Gymnasium*, but now, since he has continued with his studies at the university, where I am not allowed to go, he has passed me by" (p. 48). To what degree might Dora's maladies stem from the limited opportunities available to women of her era?

6. Although most of their romantic relationships are heterosexual, both Dora and Freud experience a strong attraction to someone of the same sex. Do you agree with Freud's view that all humans are innately bisexual?

7. "[A]s [Freud] writes up the case he is increasingly aware that he has failed this girl" (p. 185). Do you agree? Why or why not?

8. Did Freud simply use Dora to further his own career? What leads you to your conclusion?

9. Throughout the novel, Kohler strongly foreshadows the coming Holocaust and its consequences for both Freud and Dora. How does this affect the way you read their stories?

10. Freud waits five years to publish his book about Dora. He thinks that once she is married, "his time with her will no longer have the same importance it did initially. This son will replace the other men in her life" (p. 207). Does having a child somehow neuter Dora's memories of Freud?

11. Discuss the relationship between literature and psychology. How has Freud influenced the way we think about and discuss literature?

12. How well do you believe Kohler captures the nature of Freud and Dora's relationship? Have you read Freud's *Dora: An Analysis of a Case of Hysteria* (Available from Penguin in *The Psychology of Love* by Sigmund Freud)? Does *Dreaming for Freud* make you want to read or revisit it?

DATE DUE

*To access Penguin Readers Guides online,
visit the Penguin Group (USA) Web site at www.penguin.com.*